THE LONG HAUL   a novel   AMANDA STERN

Soft Skull Press

Brooklyn, NY | 2003

©2003 Amanda Stern

Distributed by Publishers Group West
www.pgw.com | 800.788.3123

Printed in the USA

Cover Photograph: Adam Kurnitz
Author Photograph: Steve Wiley
Book Design: David Janik

Soft Skull Press
71 Bond Street
Brooklyn, NY 11217
www.softskull.com

Library of Congress Cataloging-in-Publication Data

Stern, Amanda.
  The long haul / by Amanda Stern.
    p. cm.
  ISBN 1-932360-06-9 (pbk.)
  1. Young women—Fiction. 2. Man-woman relationships—
Fiction. 3. New York (State)—Fiction. 4. Codependents—
Fiction. 5. Alcoholics—Fiction. 6. Musicians—Fiction. I. Title.
PS3619.T4777 L66 2003
813'.6--dc22

                                    2003017560

ACKNOWLEDGEMENTS

The following stories, "Gravity of a Gray World," "Every step they made," and "State of Emergency" have been reprinted here with permission of: *Salt Hill, Scriptum* and *St. Ann's Review*.

There are almost more people to thank than pages in this book. While there is no coherent order, this group of people formed the cohesion that gave this book legs. Laurie Duchovny introduced me to my agent. Chris Offutt provided some crucial early editing, advice, and enthusiasm. As did Maidi Terry who I wish would move to NY already. From start to finish Kimberly Reiss, Amelia Campbell, and Tony Arkin have made me feel secure and fulfilled, as both a writer and a friend. My brother, Eddie Stern and my sister Kara Stern read, corrected, and offered insight from the first word. I can't say enough about them; they are not made from words. Peter Kunhardt sent me Sabin Streeter who helped and encouraged me even though we had never met. My mother, Eve Stuart, armed with her friends, swooped in and made important introductions. Beth Gutcheon, Wendy Gimbel, Stephanie Guest, and Gail Monaghan gave me advice and affirmation. Alida Clemens, Meghan Kelley MacKinnon, and Bo Lauder were invaluable sources of information. My agent, Andrew Blauner, fought to the finish to sell this book and when the going got tough, he talked me down ledges and bought me dinners. He answered every email and believed in me when I thought he should just give up already. Aside from that, he's a hell of a friend.

To James Garver, who I met the night I finished the book and celebrated with a year later when I sold it. Mark Fass and Ben Schrank came through in a minute with edits and careful readings. I can't thank them enough. Mike Merrill, over wine, took my book and handed me its insides. M.J Rose answered my questions, steered me in the right path and handed me invaluable pieces of information, all free of charge. And, she pointed me to Maggie McMahon. Whom I adore.

To Soft Skull for staying punk in a commercial world. My editor, Richard Nash, taught me more about writing than grad school ever could have. Aside from that, he laughs at my jokes. Everyone at SSP has made me feel welcome and part of the in-house family. Shanna Compton is a fantastic publicist, cheerleader, and champion, any author is blessed to have her on their team. David Janik, Sarah Palermo, and Tom Hopkins designed, copy edited (or managed), and allowed me to feel snug in the skull. Adam Kurnitz came through with a camera and a wise eye to make a cover when it was just a blank piece of nothing.

As well, I am indebted to these major and mini institutions: The Writers' Room (especially Donna Brodie), The Madrid Writers' Group, The American Book Center in Amsterdam, The Tin House Writers, Conference, The Wesleyan Writers Conference, Joan and John Jakobson for their generous writing scholarship, and David Byrne.

Without the inspiration of the following authors, I might still be cleaning toilets at the yoga school: Denis Johnson, John Irving, Ethan Canin, Joan Didion, James Salter, and Carson McCullers. Thank you. My gratitude for the support and generous words of Joanna Scott, Melanie Rae Thon, Maggie Estep, Victor Lavalle. and Hal Hartley has rendered me inarticulate. Reading your words is a workout for my smile muscles. I am glee and delight.

But finally, to my family, all my parents (and I have many), my enormous brood of siblings, my amazing grandmother; the marching stomp of your support has made me feel valued, recognized, but above all, loved. Thank you.

In memory of my stepfather,
James Milton Stuart.

The first one to call my words writing.

THE LONG HAUL

Three years before we said out loud alcoholic, my breath rode Rochester's snow as icicles. We scraped the car, our girl, big blue. He let me drive plastered behind a wheel. Not our house, we laughed how easy stealing was. His panic attacks one in each ventricle. His mother ate him young as afterbirth. His singing—mournful, never about me.

SYMPATHY FOR THE DEVIL

The Alcoholic says be prepared. We are in his car, his "honey wagon," an old olive green automatic Dodge Swinger from before we were born. His gig bag is in the back seat. There are picks on the ground, strings. He says something big is gonna happen tonight. I say,

"In the world?"

He says, "No. Onstage."

He is playing the Rubical, the on-campus alternative stop for hipsters, wannabes, and other rising poseurs of the twentieth-century college scene. It's on the side of the road, next to the Genesee River. It used to be a small cabin, made from wood planks that smelled from lack of maintenance. Back in the sixties, the seventies, students used it as a political activist center. They wanted to be down like the Students for a Democratic Society, but they couldn't get with the violence, so it ended up a protest house. People rallied for Angela Davis, the Chicago Seven. It burned down one night, taking with it a girl named Rubi and her boyfriend, Cal. The administration built it back up using cement and cinder blocks. It's not lovely to look at, but it's a place to go just the same.

The Alcoholic is playing his first solo gig of the year. The world, it seems, knows it. We spent the better part of Sunday hanging up flyers in town and on campus. Some folks gave him the thumbs up, others yelled, "We'll be there." I knew he was good, but I didn't see what the big deal was, why everyone wanted to go. I had never even heard his band play before. Others did. They had a huge following. Even the locals came out to hear Mr. Lipstick play.

He pops open a can of Genesee beer, drinks the whole thing in a couple swallows, tosses it to the back seat. He opens another, repeats the performance. It's near five. We're late for the sound check, but he doesn't seem concerned. I open his guitar case, run my fingers lightly across the strings. A delicate echo of notes fills the front seat.

"I had this girl once. Said my hands played her like a guitar," he offers.

"That's nice," I say.

We are in the beginning stages of our romance. He says things like this from time to time, trying to impress me. Once he told me he made it with his camp counselor at thirteen. He wants me to think he's hot shit, but I already think that. Someone taps the car window— his side. He looks up, rolls it down.

"What's up, man?" his friend asks.

"Not a whole lot," the Alcoholic responds.

"You, uh, playing tonight?"

"Yeah. You gonna be there?"

"Wouldn't miss it. Is it gonna be like last time?"

"No way, man. It's gonna be different. Really different."

"That's cool, man. That's cool."

It's bitter cold, winter already, although it's only October. The Alcoholic rolls his window back up, looks at me.

"Think I should play the black guitar or the red guitar?"

"The black guitar," I answer.

"That's exactly what I thought. We are such a good team."

He sticks a cigarette in his mouth, pushes in the car lighter, bounces his leg. He has a lot of nervous energy. Burns it right off with the leg bounce. That's why he's so damn skinny, he says. Two things I have never seen him do in the three weeks we've been together: eat and go to the bathroom.

His pea coat is falling apart. There are holes in his black jeans. The red union suit he wears underneath is too big and it bulges over the top of his pants like a beer belly. He is so skinny, even with long johns, his pants are still baggy. His hair is growing out of its skater cut. The sharp ledge in the back is getting long and I hope the next time he gets it cut, I'm with him. Maybe I'll just cut it myself. He looks seventeen to his twenty years. I look fifteen to mine. I guess he's right, we are a good team.

The car smell is growing on me. The leather interior has absorbed two decades of stale cigarette smoke. Gnarled guitar strings poke out of the closed glove compartment. Dried orange peels with cigarette stubs blistered into the skin of the rind sit forgotten under the front seat. The back seat is missing half its leather. The stuffing springs out like a fashionable fur vest.

The Alcoholic tunes his guitar. He doesn't need an automatic tuner, a tuning fork. He is his own equipment. He plucks each string, adjusts the tuning pegs, twists tones up and down octaves until he finds the right note. It takes all of one minute for him to do the whole guitar. He hotboxes his cigarette. Takes a final deep fast drag, bulldozes the last of the filter into the pullout ashtray and turns off the car.

We jog-walk downhill; the gust launches us like a slingshot. The wind brings out the freezing in the cold. It's probably ten degrees out here. Five below with the wind chill factor. I wish I were home on my couch with a blanket over me, watching a movie, drinking hot chocolate. It's ten past five and already it's pitch black. The air smells like burning pine, a forest fire. It's nostalgic, depressing. For a brief second I miss my childhood bedroom. The powdery rose perfume trapped in patches of quilt my grandma stitched when I was born. Sometimes I feel like a grain of magnetic dust being dragged by an overgrown pointer. I look at the Alcoholic, his guitar slung over his shoulder. We are a team.

The metal door sticks to its frame and the Alcoholic yanks it open. Inside, sound guys and fraternity boys run around setting up things. Someone is sweeping the floor. Everyone's still geared up in coats, hoods. It's a different type of cold in here, stagnant, like a meat locker. Guys look up, nod. The Alcoholic puts his gear onstage, shakes hands with the sound guy. I walk around the room, stand in the middle, watch the Alcoholic as he unzips his gig bag. He's doing Rodin below the mic, the thinker pose. He pulls out his slide, runs it like a bottleneck across the strings. He flat picks the steel strings with his right hand, dragging the slide back and forth over the same three frets. The acoustics in the room pick up the sound and everyone stops what they're doing, looks up.

He puts the strap around his neck, stands up. Lips purse into standard guitar face and he closes his eyes, skimming his hand across the strings, making her weep, making her sing. He removes the slide and his fingers whip into shapes of Ws and Vs across the bridge of the neck. His hand darts from one configuration to the next, never missing a note. For him it's nothing special, nothing planned. It's impromptu, a skipping of pebbles across a pond. There is something mythic about him up there, in his pea coat, caramel hair glowing under the stage lights. I am not the only one awed. A frat boy leans into me,

"Were you here last year?"

"No," I whisper.

"Oh man, it was awesome what he did. Something big always happens when he plays."

"What do you mean?" I ask.

"You'll see," he says.

The sound guy gives the signal and the Alcoholic leans into the mic.

"Microphone check. Check one, check two, check three."

The sound guy gives him the thumbs up, shines the spotlight only on him.

The Long Haul

We have a couple of hours and the Alcoholic wants to take it off-campus. We walk uphill toward the car, only this time he saunters, unswayed by the wind, chin pointed up toward the heavens, shoulders jutted back. His chest swells, puffs out. He preens. The sound check went well, he feels cocky, like a star.

The Old Toad is doing a half price happy hour, so we go there. The English accent sounds out of place in this town and we laugh when the bartender asks us if we want,

"A beah or hahd licka?"

We ride out the next hours at a back table nursing a pitcher. The Alcoholic runs through his set list, switches around a couple of songs, but won't tell me what he's playing.

"It's a surprise," he says.

I'm beginning to think he wrote a song for me. I wonder if it says he's starting to love me. I imagine him nervous up there, the spotlight dimming, him finding me in the crowd. He'll grin, his mouth will go a bit dry but he'll carry on.

"This is for you," he'll say. The song will be long, but simple. It will announce me to the world, declaring me like a major. He'll take his love and fling it over the cliff of students staring up at him from the edge of the stage. The chorus will be catchy, but wistful, the kind of song you either cry or make love to. I play with a lock of his hair, twirl it around my finger.

"So, what happened last time, what's the big deal all about?"

He looks away, gets a little nervous, purses his lips.

"Oh, nothing really. It's stupid."

"Tell me."

He looks back at me, gives me an apologetic smile and I take my hand out of his hair, lean back in the chair away from him, and brace myself for the worst.

"I proposed to my girl."

"Oh."

"It's not a big deal. I didn't even really mean it. I was drunk, it just came out and well, we're not married, so you know how it all turned out."

I smile, look around the bar, see if anyone overheard that I am not the only girl he's ever loved. At him, I just shrug. No big deal. So he wrote songs for someone else, so he was in love with her, wanted to spend the rest of his life with her. Big deal. Who cares.

"Hey, that's cool. I was engaged before also," I say, lying. His face drops a bit, and I feel the playing field level.

"You were?" he asks. "To who?"

"It's not a big deal, really. Let's talk about it another time."

"But, what was his name? What happened?"

"Really, let's talk about it later."

"Her name was Moe," he says. "That was my girlfriend's name. And his?"

I pause, think about all my boyfriends, and pick the one from sixth grade.

"Billy. Billy Macklowe," I say. He takes a deep breath, looks around. His eyes seem darker; he starts bouncing his leg, pulls at the splinters at the edge of the table. He flicks a rolled up piece of beer label off the table onto the floor.

"That's cool," he says, but he doesn't mean it.

It's getting time to pack it up, but suddenly he wants another round. A shot of whiskey, something hard. From my seat I watch him down a shot at the bar. He points back to his glass, the bartender refills. I contemplate going up there, telling him he shouldn't get drunk, but it's only been three weeks. I can't be ordering him around. He knocks back one more, heads over to me. Without meeting my eyes, he says,

"Let's go."

"How many did you do?" I ask.

"Just one," he says.

I don't say a thing.

I toss a couple bucks on the table; we throw on our coats and steer for the street. Outside, the Alcoholic is trying not to seem drunk. I ask if he's all right because he's navigating the ground like he's in high heels. He asks,

"Why wouldn't I be?"

"Well you had a lot to drink."

"Same as you," he says.

"I didn't do shots."

"I only did three," he says.

"You just told me you did one."

"No, I didn't."

"Yes, you did."

"Trust me, I know what I said," he snaps.

He's never snapped at me before.

The car is freezing and we shiver for a minute before even turning her on.

"You all right to drive?" I ask.

"Why wouldn't I be?" he answers.

"Never mind," I say.

"So, were you, like, in love with him?" he asks.

"Who?"

"Billy Macklowe."

"Oh, yeah. I guess."

"What happened?"

"He just wasn't right for me," I say, hoping this will end the conversation.

"What wasn't right about him?" he asks.

"Lots of things. Can we talk about this another time?"

"Was he good looking?"

"He was okay," I say.

He picks up one of my gloves from the floor. Starts tugging at the fingers.

"What about in bed, was he good in bed?"

I almost laugh picturing twelve year old Billy Macklowe naked.

"He was alright, I suppose."

I try to change the topic, guess how many people are gonna show up, and he gets high off the potential. He sings a couple of lines from a Velvet Underground song, then says,

"How'd he do it?"

"What?"

"Propose. How'd he propose?"

I groan.

"I don't know, on his hands and knees."

"On his hands and knees? Like a dog?"

"I guess."

"What an asshole," he says. Then laughs muttering under his breath, "on his hands and knees."

He's a better driver drunk than sober and I remember to keep that in mind.

The Alcoholic says something big is gonna happen tonight. I say,

"In the world?"

He says, "No. Onstage."

I imagine my girlfriends' faces when they realize the guy onstage is belting one out just for me. I picture them trying to contain their jealousy with forced grins; their cheekbones struggling to stay raised in the air. They'll wonder if anyone will ever do that for them, in front of an audience. Sing for their girl in front of strangers.

It's still cold at the Rubical, but with liquor in us already, it's not so hard to tolerate. He takes his ratty scarf off, tosses it behind the stage. The keg guys are starting to arrive and I watch them set up. I suck down the first few glasses of foam, helping them out. The Alcoholic is in the corner looking nervous. He pulls on a flask the sound guy gave him and quickly hands it back. I see his eyes dart my way, but I look down at the keg hose, pretend I'm not watching. I don't want him to feel spied on, don't want him to feel caught. From the periphery, I see him pull off another shot from the flask.

Someone readjusts the mics, the lights. The Alcoholic pours himself a beer from the keg. He bounces from side to side on his feet.

"You nervous?" I ask.

"No way, man. Not nervous at all."

He's never called me man before.

The sound guy wants to do another check, and the Alcoholic jumps up on stage as a couple of people enter, start setting up benches, a quasi ticket booth. As he takes his guitar out of its bag, he haphazardly knocks against the strings. The acoustics in the room pick up the sound. The crash of accidental chords carries over our heads. It's a twang, a mishap, and it doesn't sound beautiful like when his hands are sliding up and down those steel strings making even the friction sing. People look up, scrunch their noses. The Alcoholic looks around, apologetic.

Everyone's silent, listening to the mistake. The Alcoholic stands there, waiting for his cue, absorbing the silence, shifting back and forth on stage. He does not look at home. Finally the sound guy gives him a signal. The Alcoholic leans into the mic, says,

"Microphone check . . . " but there is feedback as he speaks, a loud sudden screeching from the bowels of the mic. The unexpected noise throws him and his voice turns awkward, embarrassed. He steps back. The resound dies with his retreat. The silence that follows styles him self-conscious, inorganic. In the back, the sound guy focuses on the levels; he can't see the Alcoholic becoming aware of his own skin, his sudden clumsiness.

The Alcoholic cuts into the quiet with,

"Do I look good, honey?"

I smile and shake my head yes. I like when he calls me honey. We've been going out three weeks and already he has a pet name for me. The sound guy gives him the thumbs up. The Alcoholic smiles. The sound guy looks annoyed, gives him the thumbs up again.

"Thanks, man," the Alcoholic says into the mic.

"No, kid," he says. "You need to go louder on the mic. Try it again."

"Oh," he responds.

The Alcoholic is embarrassed for misinterpreting the signs of a sound guy. He is flustered, not only being called kid, but for feeling like one. I don't really care. That's my boy up there, and soon all the girls on and off campus are going to be swaying under him.

He disappears to the bathroom. He's gone a long time and I wonder if he's changed his mind, fled. I'm almost prepared to ferry my way into the boys' room, flush him out, but he returns, edgy and disoriented. He's a new boyfriend, so I don't know whether to approach him or leave him alone. I approach, he says,

"Leave me alone."

He does jumping jacks in the corner and I'm starting to understand about stage fright. First small clusters of people arrive: the hippies, the crunchies, then larger groups: fraternity brothers, sorority sisters, punks, skater kids, techno freaks. The Alcoholic has assembled a

United Nations of college kids. Everyone wants to see him perform. Last time the stunt was about another girl, but tonight I think it'll be about me. I feel cocky that he is so cool. Like I have something to do with it.

The ambient music is Bob Dylan and people are swaying back and forth over their plastic beer cups. The Alcoholic goes behind the plate glass window, starts talking shop with the sound guy. He rocks back and forth on his feet, hands in pockets. Occasionally he takes a hand out, bites a nail, turns his head, spits it somewhere on the ground. He laughs hard a few times. Throws his head back when he laughs, leans his whole body back like he's gonna fall, but then he tips forward, tilts his head down like he's looking at his shoes. He looks up at me from time to time behind the plate glass window. Looks up at me, winks and shines a dimple or two. I think he's starting to calm down.

Everyone is still in their coats. Scarves are tied around necks; some girls have them wrapped around their heads like turbans. A group of sophomores find a spot under the stage. They stand huddled like a bunch of groupies and I feel embarrassed for them, superior. Two of the Alcoholic's friends walk in, wave to me. My roommate shows up, stakes her claim beside me. Her glasses are too large for her face and the spots of cover-up on her acne are not sufficiently rubbed in. She crosses her arms across her chest, stares at all the people, then back at me. Asks,

"You psyched?"

"Yeah," I say.

"I heard he's amazing," she says.

"Yeah," I say. "I'm sure he is."

"You know what happened last time, right?" she asks.

"Yeah," I say.

"Think he's gonna do something for you?"

I shrug and smile without saying the words, but she can tell just by looking at my grin, that yes, I think he will.

People are milling around, more and more people are crowding the stage. Some people sit. The smell of pot floats by us. My roommate smiles uncomfortably. She doesn't go out much. Everything makes her nervous. She wears a baseball cap at all times, makes sure her face is always hidden. Her sweaters hang loose and huge over her jeans, down to her knees. Makes her look bigger than she already is.

"Think they'll start soon?" she asks.

"Don't know," I answer.

It annoys me that she can't relax, that in every social situation she makes others uncomfortable simply because she is so uneasy in her bones. It seems whatever she says is irritating, even if she's telling me I look pretty. She isn't cool like I am cool, like the Alcoholic. She is academic. Acapathetic, the Alcoholic once said.

The lights start to dim and people get quiet. Some start to clap, then everyone follows. Soon we are hooting and hollering, screaming the Alcoholic's name. After a wait of three or five minutes, the Alcoholic jumps onstage in his pea coat, honeycomb hair falling in his face. The crowd jumps up and down and I can feel the vibrations of the floor below me. It reminds me of the house I grew up in. How every time the subway passed underground, the rooms would shake. I like that they are making the ground shudder for the Alcoholic.

He leans into the microphone.

"How y'all doing?" he asks.

There is feedback as everyone screams. The Alcoholic lifts his head, motions to the sound guy to turn down the volume. The anticipation is spawning butterflies in my stomach. I can barely contain my excitement at being the one he sings to. Tonight, I am the rock star's girlfriend.

"Glad y'all could make it," he says as people start to quiet down. He tunes his guitar, but somehow screws it up and has to start from scratch. He strikes the low E, but it answers him back too high, too precious. He keeps turning the silver peg, striking the note, but the pitch is all wrong. He can't get the E in its place. People start to shuffle; it's all taking too long. I know something is terribly wrong when he kneels down, pulls a tuner out of his gig bag. With its help he brings the low E into its proper pitch. He stands, relieved. He positions his hand into a bar chord, goes to strike, but the pick drops out of his hand. Just slips to the floor like a drunk. He sounds his nervous laugh, pushes three tones out from the back of his throat like a grunt. People are silent, waiting. He shakes his hands out like they're numb, shifts in his feet, back and forth, back and forth, like he has to go to the bathroom. Someone in the back yells, "You're drunk."

Again, the Alcoholic pulls out the nervous laugh.

"Yeah," he comebacks. "Just like your grandfather."

Everyone laughs, relieved. Even me. My roommate leans into me, "Is he drunk?" she asks concerned.

"No," I defend him. "Not at all. He's nervous."

"Oh," she says.

I'm thinking that broke the ice because finally he starts playing. It's a song I recognize, which is strange because the Alcoholic doesn't play covers. He sings all original songs. But this is a Stones song, a favorite: "Sympathy for the Devil." He plays a few bars, then a few more, dragging it out when he should be singing the words already. He just keeps strumming the same chords over and over again: E, D, A / E, D, A / E, D, A. People start chattering a bit, talking out of boredom, anticipation. Someone yells,

"Play the fucking song."

The Alcoholic gives an unstable smile, keeps repeating the same chords over and over until people start having whole conversations. After a full five minutes of this, the Alcoholic stops playing, looks out at the crowd, leans into the mic.

"I'm trying to play some music. If you want to talk, go to a fucking library."

"So play the song already," the same guy yells.

I'm getting nervous. Slightly embarrassed. What the hell is going on? What is he doing? Soon everyone is yelling at him to play the song. So many people are screaming that he looks like he's about to implode. I'm not sure what to do, whether I should stay put, or go up there, calm him down. He starts strumming again, the same chords over and over and over. His dead eyes stare right above the audience, at some spot no one can see. Just when I'm about to go talk to the sound guy, figure what we should do here, he starts singing.

Thing is, he's not really singing, but talking, telling a story over the chords. Soon a couple of people look up, then everyone stops talking, looks up. It takes us all a minute to realize what's happening, what he's saying.

He's revealing his dark personal history to the tune of Sympathy for the Devil. He poetry slams his secrets rhythmically over the chords. Each tale is worse than the one before. There's one about his father locking him in a closet for the night, another about his mother chasing him around with a kitchen knife because she didn't like her Christmas present. They are almost unbelievable, but somehow coming out of his mouth, you wonder. Maybe they're true.

"And I was five when my Uncle John had his moment of disgrace and shame. Made damn sure the lights were out. Undid his pants before he sealed my fate."

The audience is getting uncomfortable, they're shifting. He sings a verse about finding the body of his older sister hanging from a noose outside her boyfriend's split-level. He unveils each bloody secret with the verse: *Pleased to meet you. Hope you guess my name. But what's puzzling you is the nature of my game.*

No one moves. They stand riveted as golf tees, staring at the Alcoholic, the bloody car accident on the street. People are looking at each other, checking their watches, picking at invisible scabs, anything to refocus their attention. A girl in the corner keeps shaking her head no, no, no, as if listening makes her complicit in his history.

But he doesn't stop.

I look around, watch as a brave couple in the back sneak out the side door. Off to the side a girl picks her jacket up from the ground, a guy slings his knapsack over both shoulders.

People are whispering. Some look scared. I wonder when he's gonna play the song for me. When's the big thing going to happen? The sound guy isn't even listening, he's just making sure there's no feedback, that the levels are right, because when I catch his eye he just smiles, gives me the thumbs up.

Soon it's too much, he's gone too far, and the things he says makes people turn like milk. People don't care anymore about form, and the rustling of movement has begun in earnest. I see even his friends nod to each other, nudge their chins toward the door.

The Alcoholic strums a couple more chords. Then with no warning, he stops, lifts the strap off his shoulder, drops the guitar on the ground. It lands with a dull thud on his gig bag and a couple of dead notes vibrate on the ground. He looks out at the audience in a drunken glaze, gives us all the finger, then walks off stage, and out the door. Everyone is silent. The lights are still off, and people start talking, shooting me looks like it was me up there. I feel embarrassed for him, for me. Friends pass each other underground stares. My roommate turns to me.

"What was that?" she asks.

"I have no idea," I answer.

A couple of his friends walk over to me.

"He okay?" they ask.

"I don't know," I answer.

"Don't you think you should go after him?" his friend asks, judging me for standing there, just like him.

"I guess."

But I don't want to go after him. I am only three weeks old to him. His other friends are more than two years, shouldn't they go? I don't even know the surface of the stories he told on stage, and somehow I feel like he sold out. Shared his past with the whole world, like it had to be witnessed by others to make its point. Not just with me alone, the person it should count to most. I thought it was gonna be about me this time. But it wasn't about me. It wasn't about me at all.

People start to leave.

"Good luck," some murmur as they pass me by.

"Take it easy," others say.

The air is crisp, and I fold my arms across myself in the dark. The car is parked fifty feet away and I walk toward it slowly, reluctant. Empty beer cans and bottle caps litter the floor of the "honey wagon." There are burn holes in the beige floor lining, but these are the only signs of him here. I am relieved he's not in the car, that I can give up the hunt before it's started, but the guilt migraines me because I think I made this happen. It was my lie that undid him. If he only knew Billy Macklowe was a twelve-year-old boy whose mother still dressed him in sailor suits.

On the way back to the Rubical I am led to the pier off the

Genesee. He's sitting there at the end, legs dangling over the side, smoking a cigarette like it's a joint. I join him, keep my arms crossed.

"You alright?"

"I guess," he says. He tosses the cigarette into the river, looks away from me.

"You wanna go back in there, get your stuff?"

"No."

I'm not sure what to say so we sit for a good while, silent, overwhelmed by the sounds our own voices might make.

"What do you want me to do?" I finally ask, confused.

He stands, walks down the dock away from me. At the edge, he turns, looks at me, says,

"I want you to love me."

He jumps off the dock, onto land, but doesn't go back to the Rubical. His answer makes me feel more alone than before, but I don't know why. The river is quiet; the clouds are all black, and the only noise I hear is in the distance. The door of the Dodge Swinger opens, slams shut, but he doesn't start the car.

Inside the Rubical, the sound guy is looking for me. When I walk in, he approaches, stands there awkwardly with the gig bag, hands it to me like it's an infection.

From onstage, I watch people filter out. I roll cables, unplug amps. I'm wondering if the Rubical was always bad luck. I put the guitar gently back in its place, load the picks up into the side pocket. I zip the bag and stand up, draping its strap over my shoulder. The guitar lies across my back and for a moment I feel like a star.

The spotlight is still on. I stand in its center, let the yellow warmth drip on my face. I tap the mic; it echoes. The juice is still flowing and I lean in, expecting feedback, but I don't get the hiss. "Microphone check. Check one, check two, check three," I say shyly into the mic. My voice fills the Rubical, pours itself into every available corner, bounces itself off all the walls. The sound guy looks at me, smiles. He gives me the thumbs up and then dims the house lights all the way down.

THE LONG HAUL

The Alcoholic is behind the wheel. I'm a day done with college; he's a year. We've been on the road barely four minutes. There is a seven-hour drive ahead of us. It took two days to pack. It'll take three to undo it. The Alcoholic waited one year for me so he could leave. His other friends barely waited for their diplomas before they fled, but not the Alcoholic. He waited, hovered, and pounced when I earned my degree. We drive out of this town, me and the Alcoholic, and go South. We go South to the city where I am returning and he is following.

I don't know he is sick. His drinking has only started problems; it hasn't become the problems. I have a sinus infection made worse by tears. I have been crying, suffering from post-partum, end-of-therapy depression. I tried to stay together. I tried. But the Therapist, he wouldn't have it.

"You're too attached," he said.

"I'm not."

"You are. You need to let go."

"We could have phone sessions."

"I don't do that."

"You haven't done that."

"You need to let me go. This will be important for you. It will be good for you. It will be good."

It was not good.

We are driving out of this town—college is a day behind me and all I miss is the Therapist and that room. The chair I sat in was chocolate leather with bumps in the folds of the arms. I'd push them down when thinking, or trace the wrinkles in my jeans when avoiding an answer. A soft, tacky watercolor of a unicorn flying through a rainbow hung over his desk. I forgave him that because I liked him so much. The bookshelves were a repository for self-help titles like, *You Just Don't Understand*, *The Road Less Traveled*, and *Codependent No More*. He is an on-campus therapist, the free kind they assign when you walk in with problems. He is a graduate student at my university, in for his Ph.D., and I came with his course requirements. Part of the syllabus was reading me. He is young, early to mid thirties and ugly, but I loved him.

His sneakers lie waiting under his desk next to a yellow sports Walkman, and sometimes I imagined him at the gym playing basketball or swimming. I was jealous of those sneakers, jealous of his Walkman. Sometimes I even followed him. I called him once or twice, maybe three times. I called him quite a bit, hung up when the woman answered, lingered when he did. I loved him the way you love a father. I wanted him to save me, but he didn't. He let me go, and I wasn't near ready.

I am driving out of this town with the Alcoholic. He turns up the volume on Jane's Addiction, bobs his head and sings along, *Jane says, I'm done with Sergio, he treats me like a rag doll.* And me, I stare straight ahead, deadpan out the windshield, wondering if my sinus infection might be cancer, if a letter a day to the Therapist is too much and why when I look at my boyfriend I only see a set list.

The U-Haul we have rented is holding on to the car like a water skier, and back there everything of ours is already living together. I want to live with the Alcoholic. I don't want to live with the Alcoholic. I want to live with the Alcoholic. I don't want to live with the Alcoholic. He is chain smoking and pacing, his only form of exercise. I am packing my room up in boxes. Graduation is seventeen hours away.

"I want us to live together," he says, sprinkling ashes on the floor.

"We already talked about this."

"I want to talk about it again."

"Can I have a cigarette?" I ask.

He looks at the soft pack in his shirt pocket.

"I don't have any left."

I lean over, look in his shirt pocket into the soft pack, and count the filters.

"Yes, you do."

"You never buy your own," he says.

"So?"

"They cost money."

He reaches into the soft pack and flings one at my face. It whacks my cheek, splintering.

"You broke it. Why do you always break things?" I ask.

"Why do you always say always?" he counters.

I tear off a small piece of the packing tape with my teeth. Carefully mend the broken cigarette. I hold it up for show. He shakes his head, says,

"Always fixing things."

He sits on the box marked "Stuff From Under My Bed" and begins kicking a dent into "Junk from Desk Drawers." The regularity of the thud is meant to annoy me so I turn my back and unsuccessfully roll my futon into a cylinder. It springs back, hits me in the face.

Thud. Thud. Thud. Thud.

I pick up a box to put in the hallway, but it's too heavy for me to lift. I look at the Alcoholic who sits picking a week-old scab on his elbow. He tosses the crusted shell on the floor. His elbow starts to bleed; narrow red carpets of blood unspool down his arm. In the bathroom, I prowl the roommate's side of the cabinet. I grab rubbing alcohol, cotton swabs. I return, move his hand out of the way, dab his elbow with weeping cotton.

"I want us to live together," he whines.

"I know you do, but we already made a decision."

He flinches.

"No, you decided. You always decide. How would you like it if I just went and made a decision you didn't like?" he says. "Like . . . maybe I won't move to New York with you after all."

I press the swab into the wound hard and let it stick there. The Russian Propaganda poster he gave me is the only remaining scrap on the wall, and I walk away from him, stand under it. I fold my arms across my chest.

"Are you seriously pulling out? Is that what you're doing?"

He kicks "Junk from Desk Drawers" and stares down.

"I don't want to move to a new city if I can't live with you," his voice breaks as he says this. "It doesn't make sense. If we're both going, why waste two rents when I'll be at your house every night anyway. It's a waste of money. It's a waste of my money."

"What does that mean? Does that mean you're not coming?"

"Maybe," he says, triumphant.

"Oh come on. This is ridiculous. So I'm not ready to live with you. Big deal. That shouldn't change anything."

"It doesn't. It proves it," he says, smug, like my uncertainty is something he should be proud of.

"Proves what?"

"It proves that I love you more than you love me. If you loved me the way I love you, we wouldn't be having this conversation."

"You know how much I love you? Tell me how much. Enough to bake a cake or just a cookie?"

"I know I love you unconditionally and you don't. I know I can't live without you and you can. I know I would choose you over a career and you wouldn't. I already know."

Out the window the campus bus pulls away. I fix my eyes on the sidewalk as if maybe the right words are on Alexander Street. People have been walking around for days in their caps and gowns and it's making me feel lonely. Everywhere I look I'm seeing for the last time: the library, the bookstore, the commons. Everything is dying and I'm scared I'll be buried when I leave here. The Alcoholic claims he has no roots in any city, and even though I do, I can't find them. He gets up, goes to the futon. I think he's going to lie down, give up altogether, but he rolls it. Ties it with twine and sets it against the wall. He starts stacking the boxes on top of each other, carries them into the hallway. I put out my cigarette, look at the Alcoholic and say,

"You're wrong."

He looks up, tears plunging below him and says,

"Prove it."

The cigarettes are running low and he starts smoking the stubs from the pullout ashtray. I close my eyes like I'm poolside, feel my cheeks toast and smell the baked sun. He turns up the volume and sings along. *Jane says, I'm done with Sergio, he treats me like a rag doll.* The song is on a manual loop. He keeps rewinding before it can reach the end.

We pass Dunkin Donuts, Perkins, The Bug Jar. The Alcoholic pulls into the 7-Eleven parking lot, bolts out, returning with a fresh pack of cigarettes. We catch a red light at Meigs Street, which is a good omen, because it's the Therapist's block. I crane my neck to catch a final glimpse of his house. I have passed by it many times before. A woman's smoking a cigarette, reading the paper on her porch. A couple of kids ride their bikes toward me down the street. A teenage boy and his girlfriend soap down a car, and I imagine them tonguing each other during the radio commercials. I find the Therapist's yellow house and in my head, I lasso it, dragging it with me. Even though I am the one leaving this town, it feels like the Therapist is leaving me.

Wegmann's Grocery Store, Spiro's Charcoal Pit, Charlie's Frog Pond, Cheesy Eddie's, and Breugger's Bagels shrink in the background. I watch our history taper out the side windows. The Alcoholic stares straight ahead. Something in me is dying and I am grieving every passing gravestone.

I roll down my window completely, stick my head out and take in the freshness of upstate's air. I reach my arm out, cup my hand slightly, holding pockets of wind as we pass. I like the way it feels, like I am touching a part of the world that doesn't exist when you stand still. We pass Letchworth State Park and Crittendon Road. The concrete opens up into highway and we are flying on I-490 going east.

Jane says, I'm done with Sergio, he treats me like a rag doll. He plays the steering wheel like drums and I remember when we first met I could have listened to him play a steering wheel forever. He pushes the car lighter in; I put a cigarette in his mouth. It pops out, ready to blaze. I withdraw it, light his cigarette. The first smell of the day is smoke from a Camel Light and there is nothing, nothing warmer than nicotine burning a day out. We strap on our seatbelts, crack our knuckles, lock the doors. He turns the volume up on the song, presses a button to his right and all the windows in the back go down. I slide down in my seat, flick off my shoes and watch the white lines in the road converge on the highway's horizon.

"So, how do you feel?" he asks.

"Like shit. My head is heavy."

"I meant to be done. How does it feel to be done with school?"

"It's only been a day."

"I know, but can't you feel the freedom?"

"Yeah," I say. But I can't and I wonder what is wrong with me.

I look into each passing car hoping to find the Therapist catching up with us. He'll wave to me, gesturing in some way that lets me know being with me is more important than playing shrink to broken college kids at Mall Rat University. The Alcoholic is biting and sucking the filter like a pacifier, a nipple. The cigarette has long since burnt out, and he swings the stub with his tongue side to side like a toothpick.

"I'm thinking we could get a loft, like in Soho or something," he says.

"I don't know, I think that's out of our price range."

"Well maybe in Chelsea then."

"Same difference."

He's silent for a minute, then, "What's your problem?"

"What? Nothing."

"You're like . . . being difficult. You said you wouldn't be difficult about living together, you said you'd give it a try."

"I know, I just . . . I don't feel well. My head hurts, it's heavy."

"Yeah, you said that already."

The Alcoholic pulls into the Exxon station and we sit in a halo of yellow sunlight. Other cars pull in. Husbands and wives. Children and dogs in the backseats. Wedding rings gleam on fingers and my chest tightens looking at the gold bands. I wonder if the Therapist is married. I wonder if the woman who answers his phone is his girlfriend, his roommate, his wife, his sister. I try and remember if yellow mucus is worse than green. Infection or bacterial? Virus or disease? I lean my head back relieving my forehead of pressure, the space between my eyes, my nose.

I pretend sometimes the Therapist is watching me. Like he's viewing the developments of my life as they're occurring, like a movie, a polaroid. I pretend he can see me on his television monitor sitting in this gas station in this car waiting for the Alcoholic. Believing he's watching me helps me feel safe. Sometimes I daydream that he takes me in. We set up the TV room as my own and at night he comes in, plays his ear as a stethoscope to my chest, makes sure I'm still breathing. On weekends he wants to know where I'm going, when I'm coming home. If I'm late, he'll worry, call the police.

The Alcoholic fills the tank, ducks into the quik-mart for a six pack of Genesee, another carton of Camel Lights. On his way back he tosses me a packet of Bambu rolling papers. I pop open the glove compartment, pull out the ancient bag of pot and roll a smooth hard joint on my lap using an old guitar magazine as surface. I hand it to him when I'm done.

"You don't want any?" he asks.

I shake my head. He passes me a beer, but I don't want that either.

"What's the matter?"

"Nothing. I just don't want a beer."

"Are you mad at me?" he asks.

"No. I just want to sleep."

"You sure you're not mad at me?" he says.

"Yes."

"I love you," he says, like it's a question.

I smile.

"Do you love me?" he asks.

"Yes monster, I love you."

"What's the matter? Are you mad?"

"I'm not mad. I just don't feel well. I'm sick, remember? I just want to sleep."

"Okay, don't be mad. Go to sleep. We'll stop for some medicine soon, okay?"

I nod.

"I love you," he says.

I close my eyes, turn my face away from him. I breathe deeply, trying to locate the exact site of sinus pain. I color it red and throbbing, picture it turning orange than yellow than white than gone. But, it's not gone, the pressure. It's not gone at all. The Alcoholic starts mumbling, talking. I keep my eyes closed; I don't respond. I try to fade him out, but he keeps chattering. Something about the recession, the worst economy in blah blah blah and then something else about the baby boomers. I open my eyes, face him.

"I am trying to sleep," I say.

"Well, what about me?" he says. "It's not fair I have to drive the whole seven hours and can't even talk to you."

"Just give me a half hour," I say. "Can you do that?"

He is quiet for about two minutes. He turns on the radio, flicks the knob to static, then through grabs of music . . . white noise . . . talking . . . debating . . . music . . . white noise . . . talking . . . debating. He stops on a political talk show. I open my eyes again.

"Please," I beg.

He flicks it off angrily, starts humming, then singing. I open my eyes. I glare at him. He swallows the lyrics. I face the window, shut my eyes again, trying my hardest not to get worked up, to relax so I can just fall asleep, drift, make my sinus headache ease up, go away. He starts muttering under his breath, talking to himself. I make out patches of words: the Truman Doctrine, Trust Busting, the Socialist party. He is lecturing the car, progressively getting louder.

There is no use; there will be no sleeping. Without alerting him, I open my eyes to watch the countryside skim past from the side of the world. Snapshots of my life whip past me like billboards: youth, adolescence, grown-up, burnout. A trucker keeps a doggy-paddle pace beside our car. He winks at me, spreads two fingers in a V and wags his tongue between them. I do nothing. He speeds on.

The car is filling with pot smoke and I half pray for a contact high. I'll miss the late nights on the Alcoholic's front porch smoking pot, drinking forty ohs. Jimmy Giuffre playing jazz guitar on vinyl in the background; hearing the record needle play each groove; skim the surface of scratches. Trees, the smell of winter. Washing the car to music on a hot day. Wrapping ourselves in sleeping bags and thawing out beside a fire. Listening to the Alcoholic sing and play guitar like we're sitting around a campfire. Eavesdropping on his political conversations that make no sense to me. Historical debates I can't follow. I miss the days before we needed each other. He is leaving his element. We are driving toward mine.

The Alcoholic is humming, drumming, driving at cruise control. He turns up the volume and sings along. *She gets mad and she starts to cry takes a swing but she can hit!* His voice is worn down and raspy from smoking, but underneath the wear and tear is an innocence, a soft skull on a grown man's head. He can harmonize anything, even instruments. It doesn't matter the music: punk, metal, grunge; listening to him sing is a mindful experience. *I'm gonna kick tomorrow . . . I'm gonna kick tomorrow.* I shut my eyes and he's singing for me.

The Therapist asked what I loved about the Alcoholic. I told him when the Alcoholic is on stage singing, I want him bronzed. I want his face in all available colors. To show him off glossy, matte, sepia toned. He is photogenic, better looking than I will ever be, maybe he'll even be a star, and somehow, that is deeply significant.

"Why is that so important?" the Therapist would ask.

"I don't know," I would always say.

And the Therapist would answer,

"You can do better than that."

Sometimes he cries when driving and I make him pull over because his eyes fog over from tears. I make him turn down the volume on Jane's Addiction, because melody makes him worse and we pull off at Seneca Falls. He flicks the key and the car abruptly dies. He tells me he feels safe with me, that he wouldn't know what to do without me, that I am the only person in the world who cares about him, believes in him. If I ever left him, he'd die, that's for sure, he says. He'd walk into traffic, fill up a bathtub, hang his own head. He says I am the only one who understands him. Am I in this for the long haul? Like really? Do I love him enough to deal with his shames? Because he's damaged and I'm the only one that can heal him. Will I leave him? He means ever. Am I permanent? Because he needs to know right now . . . just tell him, tell him that I'm in for the long haul, like forever.

"Yeah. I'm in."

"You sure? Because you sure don't sound sure."

"I'm sure."

"Because if you're not sure you should just tell me now."

How can anyone be sure about the future, the long haul? Sometimes you feel like you are submerged, like you are looking at the sky through water. You know you don't belong there, but it's warm and safe and although you wish you had courage to make it on land, see the sky through your own eyes, not through the swells, the crests—you don't. You stay. You understand somehow that you are settling and no matter how close you get to surfacing, you never do. You are waiting, waiting for someone to save you, waiting for the Therapist. You watch your life from the bottom of a rivulet. It unfolds before you in the second person.

"Well, I'm not entirely sure," you say.

Long pause—his now.

And then, the tears. They come out as rocking sobs. Shuddering his entire body and taking with it my guilt for having caused him this. I see him plummet, falling below all surfaces. His wails are long and uninhibited. His mouth, like a jack is wedged in there, is racked wide open. I said once I'd never hurt him, but look at me now. I go to him slow, hand first, then arm, and he retreats, pulls back—recoils. He retreats and I go to him. He withdraws and I go to him because I know this is what he wants. The Therapist said the Alcoholic needs saving. Between sobs:

"You don't love me?" he asks.

"I do. I love you."

He puts his head on my lap and I rock him back and forth, soothing him like a baby.

"Then what? What's wrong?"

"Nothing's wrong. I just . . . why do we have to talk about this now?"

"Because...because I need to. I need to know."

"What do you need to know?"

He sits back up.

"Whether you're in this for the long haul."

"Why do you make it sound so unattractive?"

"I don't."

"You do. The long haul? Long haul? What's attractive about that?"

"You know what I mean."

"I don't."

"Forever. Are you in this forever?"

My head is throbbing; we are not getting closer. Closer to the city, closer to medicine. We are just here. Stuck. Stuck in a big car in a small town whose sign reads Cayuga and wobbles a bit with the wind. Someone is cutting his or her lawn and it smells like the wheat grass from Lucky's Juice Joint. I want to marry the Alcoholic. I don't want to marry the Alcoholic. I want to marry the Alcoholic. I don't want to marry the Alcoholic. The Therapist told me the color of leaves is most brilliant just before they die.

"I'm moving to New York for you," the Alcoholic says.

"What's that supposed to mean?"

"I wouldn't have come if I thought this was temporary."

By the side of the lake a woman piggybacks her boyfriend. She runs with him, spins him round and round until the lines between them merge and they become one person. He can't see his own feet, and hers are starting to blur.

"My whole life is packed up in the back of this car and you don't know if you want me?" he says.

"I never said that."

"You basically did."

"You're twisting my words around," I say.

"You're twisting my emotions around," he says.

I want medicine. I want to feel better. If I feel better, I'll know what to do, have the right words to say what I want. But now, my head is clogged and I feel unreal. I am stuck two miles off the highway watching his life become mine, waiting for his stoned red eyes to turn blue again. The sun falls dry on my face and I expect it to tear me apart.

On the lake there are families. People on rafts, men fishing. There are children in bathing suits that are too small for their pudgy bodies, teenagers sitting on picnic tables hating every second of every second. The car windows are rolled down all the way and the air smells clean like a fresh scrubbed face. The lake's surface is calm and underneath that, it's calmer. The kids jumping in off the side of the docks are the only ones to make a dent in the water. Ripples move away from them, toward us and flatten before reaching the shore.

"Don't you want that?" he asks.

"What?"

"A family. Don't you want a family?"

"Yes."

"With me?"

"Well someday. Probably."

"Probably? What's that supposed to mean?"

A little girl laughs, tossing her head back so her blonde ringlets fall behind her. Her father is making faces at her. The mother is wiping her forehead, reading an issue of Ladies Home Journal and looking periodically out toward the horizon. She is worried. She gets up, walks to the edge of the water. She stands there, lost in her own anxieties, fears. She turns back to her husband, her daughter, but doesn't seem to see them. They are invisible, overlooked.

"I want that," the Alcoholic says. "With you."

The Alcoholic pops open another beer. He drinks it in four or five enormous gulps, tosses it in the back seat and pops open another can.

"You shouldn't be drinking so much," I say.

"I'm not."

"This is your third beer."

"It's a long drive."

The Alcoholic watches as the father swings his little girl around by her arms. He spins her in circles and she shrieks with laughter.

"Daddy. Stop," she yells, but she doesn't mean it.

The empty bottles of Genesee roll at my feet and he wipes his nose on the back of his sleeve. Winter is over, summer is pulling over our heads and we are itching to go somewhere. The cut grass is summer but the smell is nostalgic, the first day of school, the last day of camp. I baptized the sky mine once, but looking at it now I forget its name, and my own. I am losing four years already. I should have held on tighter. My head throbs. I can't bear the weight of it much longer. Benadryl would work, Tylenol Sinus a close second. I'd take anything to drain my head, make me sleep. I'd say anything just for him to start this car, get us where we need to be.

"I need medicine," I say, but he doesn't turn the key.

"Why did you say probably?" he asks.

"Probably?"

"About a family. You said probably."

"I didn't mean it."

"You didn't?"

"No," I say.

"So you want a family?"

"Yes."

"I mean with me."

Pause.

"Yes," I respond.

"I don't believe you," he says, but this time he starts the car.

The Alcoholic rewinds the tape, presses play. *Jane says I'm done with Sergio, he treats me like a rag doll.* There's a mall up ahead and I point to it. He pulls off the next exit. I get out but he stays in the car, bobbing his head and playing the steering wheel.

The neon overhead turns my skin green. The toilet flushes automatically; I get sprayed. My head is overcast, leaden. I am damp, sweaty;

hair is stuck to my cheeks. My skin is in blotches the shape of clouds.

I go to McDonald's. The families are small in number but gener-ous in mass. White sweatshirts, platinum hair, mall jewelry, leggings, no fashion sense. One mother drags her little boy by the collar like a dog. Another boy has a leash strapped around his belly. He trails behind his father, who momentarily lets go to peruse the "National Enquirer." A family of four sits silently in a booth. They eat in fast gulps. There is no chewing, just biting, swallowing. The mother watches the TV overhead ignoring her spouse, her kids. They kick each other under the table, smack each other over their food. A set of twins with Fetal Alcohol Syndrome sit in high chairs. Their eyes are set wide apart, pacifiers hanging just out of reach. I buy a Value Meal for the Alcoholic, a Happy Meal for myself.

The magazine kiosk doesn't have Benadryl, so I buy a generic form of sinus control and ride my way back down the escalator. I am float-ing. I am Miss America. I am Homecoming Queen. I am a junkie. The families stare at me the way I stared at them. Little kids drop jaws, lol-lipops fall out of mouths, eyes are quickly diverted, then returned. My jeans are torn, held together by patches with boys' names on them: Travis, Glenn, Frankie, Stan. My gray sweatshirt is not designer. There are no studs on it, no jewels. It is not ornamental, just functional. There are stains. My hair has formed dreds. I have cornrowed a few sec-tions out of boredom. My part has disappeared under dirt, build-up, frizz. I am not wearing makeup, not even chapstick. I am gray-green, sick, unwell, ill. I am a punk rock star, an "It" girl. I am a failure.

We stop at a cheap hotel so the Alcoholic can steal a swim in the pool. I use part of my graduation money and rent a room so I can sleep. When we get there, he decides he's too tired to swim and he lies down next to me on the bed. The sunlight seeps in through the sides of the closed curtains and the Alcoholic instantly falls asleep holding a pillow over his face like he's suffocating himself. The sinus medicine slowly drains my head, making me feel feathery. A bad spackle job roughs up the ceiling like little wakes in the ocean. The door has holes from fights down its spine. The Alcoholic's body jerks a few times like a bad actor in a death scene. This is how he sleeps—in fits and starts.

Back in the days of my insomnia, the Alcoholic would have me lay my ear to the pillow, listen for the muted pounds of my heart under the down feathers. I'd fall asleep to the thump and hammer of my own rushing blood. I listen for it now, but all I hear are soldiers marching. The tramp and strut of miniature feet.

The red light blinks on the phone with a message. I fantasize it's the Therapist. I daydream he's calling to tell me he's thought it over. He's moving to New York, starting his own private practice. He'll tell me he misses me, thinks of me, can't wait to hear everything I have to say. I watch the red blinking light nourished with the hope of him.

The Alcoholic opens his eyes after a half an hour. He stretches, arms over his head, legs slightly parted. Sleep is crusted to his eyelashes and he picks it off, tosses it to the floor. He rolls over, lies on top of me. He mashes his lips against my neck, my ear. I push him back.

"Honey, I'm sick," I say.

"Come on. I'm doing all the driving. The least you could do is give back."

He climbs back on me, pushes himself into me, rearing his tongue into my mouth. I turn my head away, he gets mad.

"Jesus what's your problem? You never want to have sex."

"That is not true. I'm sick. I don't feel well. I am unwell."

"You look fine to me."

He sits up, stares at himself in the dirty mirror.

"Don't you think I'm attractive?" he asks.

"Yes," I say.

"Then what's the problem?"

"I'M SICK!"

"Do you think that maybe you don't like boys?"

I laugh, simultaneously insulted and amused.

"Seriously. If you're a lesbian, I could deal with it. You can tell me. Otherwise, it must be me. You think I'm ugly."

"I'm not a lesbian."

"So it's me. I'm ugly."

"I don't think you're ugly."

He starts to cry.

"Yes, you do. You think I'm ugly. Otherwise you'd want me."

In a few minutes my pants are down and he's on my back, humping my ass to get off. This is our version of compromise sex. When he cums, he sighs, kisses my neck and rolls off me. He goes to clean up in the bathroom and I stare at the flashing red light. When I hear the faucet running, I pick up the phone.

"Hi," I say. "Do you have any messages for room ten?"

"You Rosita?" he asks.

"No," I say.

"Then you got nothing."

"But our red light is blinking."

"It's blinking for Rosita, not you. No messages."

Dial tone. I hang up the phone, watch the red blinking light until it suddenly stops, turns black.

The Alcoholic comes out of the bathroom wearing just his boxers. He picks his pants up off the floor, crams one leg in fast, then the other. His boxers bunch up like the bellows of an accordion but he doesn't adjust them, he doesn't seem to care. He pulls his white shirt over his head. He wears yellow rings into stains on the armpits of his ten pack K-Mart tee shirts. Clothes drape off him like he's a hanger. I can see the bones of his knees through his jeans. He wants to check out the pool but I want to rest a bit more. He tells me to come get him when I'm ready. Then he takes off for chlorinated water.

The ceiling lamp dulls to a stop. I pull the sheets off me. They are sticky with humidity. I have a staring contest with the phone but I blink first. I want to call the Therapist to tell him about the long haul, to ask him what he thinks. I want him to say,

"Don't commit to the Alcoholic. Wait for something better. Wait for me."

Maybe the Therapist can't live without me like I can't live without him. I want to ask the Therapist about the long haul. I want to know about forever. I pick up the receiver and dial the number I have long since memorized. When the Therapist answers, all I can muster is,

"Hi."

"Who is this?" he asks.

"It's me," I say.

He is silent for a second and then takes a deep breath. My stomach drops out. I need to unleash myself in the bathroom. Just hold on, I say to myself. Hold on.

"What can I do for you?"

His tone is official, like he's breaking up with me. I feel foolish, like a schoolgirl after her teacher.

"Nothing," I say.

"Don't say nothing. Tell me what you want."

I want him to stop snapping at me. I want him to miss me. I want him to worry about me. I want him to care for me. I want him to come get me.

"I want . . . I . . . I miss you."

"We've been through this," he says.

"Can we go through it again?" I ask.

"No. You need to let me go."

"I can't. It's too hard."

"You can. You have to. I need to get off the phone now."

"Don't you even miss me?" I ask.

He breathes heavy, like a prank caller.

"I wish you the best of luck with everything. Be well," he says and hangs up.

The room is dead. The mirror, the plastic plant, the ceiling fan. Nothing alive lives here. Through the green curtain the light casts a diseased hue over everything. On the last day of class, my Spanish teacher stood in front of us, her canvas skirt covered in chalk, her long yellow hands gesticulating like a conductor, and she pointed the chalk at my empty face, demanding I repeat the words: estoy sola, estoy sola. I am alone. I am alone.

There is no one in the swimming pool. A woman in her mid-forties lies on a chaise, leathery from too much sun. Her backside is lubricated with baby oil, and she lies on her front reading a tabloid. He's not in the gift shop, the front lobby, the parking lot.

The hotel bar is long and narrow, like a drawn-out yawn. The Alcoholic is the only one there. He sits at the counter talking to the bartender. They are watching a baseball game on TV. I am in the doorway, hidden, out of sight. There are two empty shot glasses beside him, and a full tank of scotch on the rocks in front of him. They are laughing, high fiving each other over the dank anemic counter. The Therapist is not going to save me. The promise of him in my future is gone. I was just another name on the roll call, another couple of syllables for his mouth to fit around. I am a statistic, a line on a graph, a bunch of symptoms in the DSM-IV. All I have is this, this pub loving boy leaning over a bar drinking scotch on the rocks, betting all his money on a game he doesn't even understand. He is all I have. Estoy sola.

In the hotel parking lot, cars pull in and out, interchangeable as batteries. He looks sexy with his cigarette in his mouth as he searches his massive chain for the car keys. He looks over at me and I catch his eyes. He smiles at me, and I know that however deep it runs for him, he does truly love me. He unlocks the car doors and we slide in.

The sun has heated the seats for us. We are halfway home. Halfway gone. Side by side we sit staring out at the hotel, the ugly beige rooms, the janitor smoking a joint by the dumpster. Even if I am not in love, I think, I have someone. Someone who wants me, someone who will always be there. Someone who might possibly save me, let me save him. I look at the Alcoholic and say,

"I'm in."

"I know, babe, we're both in."

"No, I mean, I'm in."

"What?" he says, confused.

"The long haul," I tell him. "I'm in for the long haul."

He grins, starts the car and we go. He turns up the volume on the radio and sings along. He's always singing along.

CRIME BABY

The Alcoholic is sleeping with someone in group therapy. I've seen him around, know his band is big on campus, but I never bother with him. He walks in a permanent slouch, like his shoulders surrendered to gravity. I've never seen his face, just the top of his head as it nears me. Word is he doesn't have a strong jaw. I am one of the few not dripping for him.

My current boyfriend is transatlantic and echoes on the phone. When he returns he'll go three thousand miles from me. Now, he is a year in England at some fancy college named for some crucial person I've never heard of. My current boyfriend is older, smarter, takes care of every little thing. Now I am alone, unsure of the world, scared of myself and of all the bad decisions I might make. We said we wouldn't date other people, but I am aching from the distance. Cracks are fracturing in my arms, my legs.

Academic probation takes my scholarship; dangles it right in my face. My major is making movies but I wind up just watching them instead. There are papers to write, short films to shoot, but my mind is expanding in closed-in viewing rooms. The other students are reading the theory of it, talking the frames right out of the shots, the scenes. The Professors say talking is thirty percent of your grade. I don't say a word for a good long time. Not a goddamn thing, just sit back absorbing the toxins in the projector, the flog and flutter of the reel to reel. They drop my grades like a baby on her head.

I am on work-study, working the day shift in the film library. It's there I discover Antonioni and Godard. Soon I start cutting the classes, but before then, before I give it all up, I spend the afternoons locked in black space, rooms the size of matchboxes, shooting up Neo-

Realism and the French New Wave. Work-study is signing people in, setting up chairs, pressing play on the VCRs for students with pens and paper in thick tortoise shell glasses. I can't bother with them, their freshman enthusiasm, their pretentious academic vocabulary. I want to swallow their words, bite the heads off the first syllables, watch their helpless pupils as *diagetic, iconic, syntagma, dialectic, pedagogical, codified, diachronic* flail disabled and shirtless in the wind. I can see their startled pimpled faces as I chew their inflated phrases.

I am memorizing David Hemmings's face in *Blow-Up*, Brigitte Bardot's hair in *Contempt*, Anna Karina's coy glances in *My Life to Live*. I always hear the knocking; I know they are waiting. But I lock the door, keep the lights off. I don't care about the papers they have to write, the theses they are slaving over. I care about the layers, the way the light binds people to their destiny, the gritty texture, the shaky in-your-face hand-held camera, the dirt under the nails of the characters. It leaves me breathless. I want to be street like Jean Seberg.

I don't know who calls it in, but they are getting complaints; there is talk of my scholarship being taken from me. They make me fill out forms before placing me on probation.

"You're in quite a bit of trouble, young lady . . . your education is on the line . . . there are plenty of students more than capable of replacing you . . . this is quite serious . . . there is nothing to smile at . . . this is no longer a warning," they said.

Made me sign my life away to the weekend shift. One screw-up and they are giving my work study to the fat girl with the acne scars who still plays recorder even though she isn't nine anymore. My last day before the weekend shift is spent alone in the quiet of a viewing room, memorizing Belmondo's brood, the running of his finger over his lips. There hasn't been sun on my skin for days.

I fall out of the library, trip on the sun's blaze in my face. The sky's high beams are turned all the way up, headlights blaring. I feel a deep need for a cigarette. Since they don't sell them on campus, a drag all its own, I am looking around, watching for a spare stick. I am thinking about cutting my hair short, dying it blonde. I am thinking about getting one of those striped long sleeve tee shirts Seberg wears in the film. I am thinking stuff like that when I see the Alcoholic with the carton on the floor.

He is sitting on the steps chain smoking from a crate he has book-ended on the ground between his dirty wrestling sneakers. I recognize the hair, his jagged greasy part, the tattered ends falling across his face.

"Spare a cigarette?" I ask him.

When he makes no significant move, I'm not sure he heard me, so I stand there, self-conscious as a teenage girl seeking an autograph. You can tell his eyes hurt too, because he's looking down even with sunglasses. He wears gloves with no fingers; his nails are dirty and worn. He flicks the ash off the end of his cigarette near my feet, fish-es through his pocket for some gum, scratches his arm through his thrift store pea coat. He is all hands. Finally he reaches into the car-ton, pulls an entire pack out and hands it to me. Just gives me twenty free cigarettes right then and there. Keeps his eyes to the ground the whole time.

"Thanks." I say.

He says nothing. It's Jen who tells me he is sleeping with someone in group therapy. She should know; she's friends with the girl. The girl is a grad student and seven years older than us. She calls the Alcoholic her "little boy," and hearing it then makes me sad for both of them. The Alcoholic is smoking the living shit out of the filter. The second it dies he lights another. He never once looks up. I'm not sure if it's him or me that's invisible.

A couple of days later, I get the flyer also. It's black, and in silver reads: Come as You Are. I was getting the left-out feeling; everyone else seemed to have got one days before. There is just an address and a date. No one knows who is throwing it. I guess it doesn't much matter for me; it's a Friday, and now I work the night shift. I can't stand hearing everyone talk about it, what they're gonna wear, who they're gonna bring. College is making memories and if you're absent, you're out of the loop for life. I'm scheming, coming up with ways to cut work, hire a recruit, a frosh. Nothing is panning out. My friends are going in groups, driving, taking the bus. Everyone will be there; no one will be on campus. Who would miss me? Who would even check that I was there?

The party is off-campus and my weekend friend drives me there. She's my weekend friend because she has a car. Monday through Friday I take the bus. She was the one that said she'd get me back for the second half of my shift. She's the one that said nobody rents movies on the weekend. I said weekends are for drinking, smoking, making out, raising hell and getting busted. I need to save my scholarship, so I plan on working the last hour of the shift, one to two in the morning. At nine p.m. I hang a sign on the door of the film library. It says: Back in Five.

Being she's my ride, I make sure my weekend friend understands the importance of getting me back to work by one, that it's a matter of financial importance. It's a necessity, not a favor.

"I get it," she says.

In the car she turns up the volume on her new boyfriend's demo tape, sings along with all the bad lyrics.

"He's a genius. Isn't he a genius?" she asks me.

"Yeah," I say. "The Mick Jagger of garage pop."

"Garage Pop. I like that. Hey honey, did you hear that? Maybe you should call your band Garage Pop," she says.

Her new boyfriend, Dave, a long-haired drooping pseudo-hippie who lights as bright as highlighter on skin, sits in the back smoking a joint he will learn later in the emergency room is laced with PCP, and that's why the angels are dying at his feet. I stick with cigarettes and feel just fine.

It's a three-family house at the edge of the woods. Rumor has it there's a dog that is basically good, except he's excitable, occasionally pisses in their closets. Even from inside the car we can hear the old soul leaking out from inside the brown French Colonial. When we walk in, the smell of cigarettes, pot and incense swallows us like a hit. Upstairs we hear the dog running, the scratch of his nails as he skids across the wooden floor. An old James Brown record spins, turns itself like a hula hoop round and round. People are dancing already. I make my way through the crowd to the kitchen.

There's this hot guy, like a Xerox of Jean-Pierre Leaud from *The Mother and the Whore.* His face is broken up by a prominent nose and a chin cut narrow and small. When he leans over, a tuft of thick black Bohemian hair falls over his empathic eyes. He's boiling a Chai Rum concoction while other people sit on the counter talking, smoking, moving to "Cold Sweat." I greet people, grab a plastic cup, fill it up with Genesee. My friend sees her ex-boyfriend. She lounges all over her new man, tries to make the old one jealous, but he doesn't seem to notice. Or care. Jean-Pierre Leaud passes around his brew, then runs out to dance to "Get up Offa That Thing." Someone comes in with a grab bag of bongs and bowls. I reach my hand into the pillowcase, pull out an intricately carved pipe from Thailand. Someone fills it. I smoke up. When I'm done, I stick the pipe in my pocket. No one sees me do it, and I get chills at how easy stealing is.

My weekend friend leaves me with her new drooping boyfriend, whose vocabulary consists of three words: dag, stick, and sweet. Jean-Pierre Leaud comes back, chats me up a bit, which I like because he looks like a movie star. A woman emerges from the bathroom, a regular Anna Karina. She's dark-haired, big boned, slightly ethnic. Her nose is chaffed from blowing, and toilet paper lint clings like a rumor to the canal that divides the upper lip into the M. She wraps herself around Jean-Pierre Leaud's waist, pours her head into his neck.

"Ragweed," she tells everyone.

Jean-Pierre steals away, embarrassed. She is the ex who can't let go. He doesn't want to appear taken, especially by her. In the living room he plays jazz on his guitar. I listen for a bit, sit near him. He looks at me, smiles.

"That your own stuff?" I ask.

"No," he says. "It's Jimmy Giuffre."

"It's good," I say.

"Isn't it?" he says enthusiastically.

Another girl walks in, sits down next to the hot guy, a little too close, and Jean-Pierre pushes over, away from her. Her flesh has permanent folds in it, like a piece of paper that won't lose its crease. Her neck bears faint red lines from too much looking down. Her chest is wide as a doorframe. Her waist doesn't taper. She's thick. Her energy is Junior High: trying to fit in with a crowd that never wants you. I see right through her. So does Jean-Pierre.

"Play that song I like," she says.

"No. I hate that song," he says. Jean-Pierre gets up, walks away. I glare at her for sitting down in the first place. I glare at her for living.

My weekend friend finds me, grabs my hand, and we navigate through the crowd and up the stairs. I trail behind her. Upstairs there are three bedrooms, a small study, and a bathroom. Party chatter escapes beneath closed doors, pot smoke carries and the dog barks. My friend pushes open a door with her dirty cowboy boot. Inside are patches of people. Some on the floor, some on the bed. There is the dog, a collection of overly pretty girls, a guy with a guitar, a girl with a bong. My friend looks around the room. She spots the Alcoholic sitting in a small circle, wearing his fingerless gloves, his shoddy pea coat. She says,

"You moved the bed."

Without looking up he says,

"No. It's the same."

"Really?" she says. "I could have sworn it was by the window."

"No," he says. "It was always right here."

"We were in it so much, guess I never really noticed where it was."

She laughs. He doesn't, just keeps his eyes to the ground. I back out of the room, walk further down the hall. The dog follows, trails me, then shoots ahead, disappearing into a closet.

The stairs to the attic are steep. The dust rides my throat like a cowboy. I feel around for a light switch, brush against something string-like and pull. The glow from the bulb is fading. A drum set sits center stage. Sticks are on the ground. Boxes, some open with clothes and letters spilling, pile on top of each other like a football tackle. Dead guitar parts and ratty steel strings coil in the corner. Dust particles form coronas in the light beams and dance above ground without falling. I go to the drum set, sit down on the stool. A folded letter lies out of its envelope on the snare. I open it and read:

> I get out of this place in a coupla weeks. Thinking I'll drop
> by school, make an appearance. I'm on the ninth step,
> which means I make amends now to all the people I hurt.
> You're on the list and I'm hoping you'll save me some face

time so I can make reparations. I may be the last person
you wanna see. Maybe I'm the first. You tell me. xxoo Moe

I fold it back up, knowing more than I want to, yet nothing at all. I
look up, startled to see someone staring at me from the top of the attic
steps. His skin is ceramic, smooth, like blown glass. He has outdoor
cheeks, pink and kissed. Enormous cerulean moons stand for eyes. He
smirks; dimples emerge on both cheeks. My stomach drops out a bit,
my chest compresses. I am overcome with infatuation. The crush
forms, settles in. He stuns me. His lips pucker; he shyly bends his head
down like he's the one that's been caught. I see it then, the jagged part,
the tattered ends falling across his face. Other things focus: his fingerless gloves, his ratty coat. This is the Alcoholic. I try not to stare,
which is difficult, because for the first time I am seeing his face. He is
better looking than any of the French New Wave guys. Better looking
even than Jean-Pierre Leaud. He is beautiful to me: this is his house,
he has slept with weekend friend and I have stolen his pipe.

"Hey," he says.

"Hey back," I say.

I feel wrong and out of place, like a tomboy stuffed in a tutu.
Everything I say or think sounds stupid. I don't want to talk; I just
want to look at him.

"You know how to play?" he asks.

I look down at the drums. Can he see the letter from where he is
standing? I pretend it's not there. That when I look down all I see are
drums, not this letter. I try to forget what it says, but suddenly and
inexplicably I am threatened, jealous by this person, this Moe.

"No." I say. You?"

"Yeah."

We are silent, looking at each other from across the room, and all

I want to know is did he see me reading the letter, and is it his?

"Wanna get outta here?" he asks.

He walks ahead of me. Stuffed into the back of his pants is a somewhat hefty paperback, whose title I can't make out. We pass the room with the weekend friend, a smaller room with just a desk, and a closet. As we pass, I peer inside, see the dog squatting, pissing on all the shoes.

The picnic table is still wet from old snow, but we sit on it anyway. He pulls the book out of his back pocket, lays it down next to him on the table. I lean over, look at it. Its title: *A Cinema of Loneliness*.

He tells me a story about this one Christmas when he was seven, left his house after dark, after all the yelling was done, and came upon an old man, homeless and drunk. The man gave him his first drink, got him rocked off a flask of whiskey, and when the Alcoholic was good and gone, the old man came clean as the son of God. Said his twelve apostles lay sleeping in the woods. To this day the Alcoholic believes it. Wants to go back and find him, ask him the meaning to this meaningless life.

We do what they all do, find the thread that links us. Some people start with books and movies, TV shows and plays, but not us. Our flirting is dark, heavy. We bond over the past, the bad stuff; nothing has died for us, everything hovers, still quite alive.

My story, his story. I don't want to leave him ever. You can see it in his eyes: he is broken up and thrown like a baby. I want to take it all away, take it all back even though I didn't do it. He sees it in me too, I can tell. The Alcoholic says he can see through me, says we are both the same.

"I know all about you," he says.

"What do you mean?" I ask.

"You're damaged," he says.

I don't say anything. I just look away.

"That's why I like you," he says.

"You really think I'm damaged?" I ask.

"Yeah," he says. "Just like me."

And then he is smooth.

The Alcoholic says I am Bounty, I am soaking him up. He says I am the cherry in his Shirley Temple. He says I am the hangar for his soul. If he were a battery, I'd be the juice. He says I am the arrow on his compass. He says he missed me before he knew me. I say don't piss on my back and tell me it's raining.

Our foreheads are almost touching; we stare at each other for a full five minutes or so. I don't ever want to leave this moment. The Alcoholic is pouring down on me. My weekend friend and her droopy boyfriend find us in the yard. She taps me on the shoulder.

"It's one o'clock," she says.

"Yeah," I say but don't get up.

"You have to go," she says. "You'll lose your scholarship."

"Five more minutes," I say.

She shrugs, walks away.

The Alcoholic gets his guitar, plays me a song he wrote. It's folky and catchy, and if I had it on tape I'd listen to it everyday. He tells me about the Sunday Circle he hosts in his house. No instruments allowed. Just bodies, just souls. The gathering is in the kitchen, around the rectangle wood table, on the counter, makes no difference. Each person gets a utensil, household, or kitchen. Some people play buckets like drums; others play spoons on the wall. The jam is authentic, genuine, ritualistic. It can last ten minutes. It can last three days.

If they recorded the music they made they'd all be famous by now. I want to be a part of the circle.

My weekend friend comes back.

"You ready?" she asks.

I have no desire to leave. His big eyes are wet with beer glaze. He looks away from me, disappointed. I'm inflated by a startling urge to vow I'll never hurt him.

"Do you have to leave?" he asks.

"Yeah," I say.

"She's supposed to be at work," the weekend friend says.

"I wish you could stay," he says.

"Five more minutes."

She comes back ten minutes later. Just stands there and stares at us until the Alcoholic looks up, says:

"I'll drive her."

"Yeah?" I ask.

He looks at me hard, smiles.

When we get up to leave, I take the pipe out of my pocket, place it gently on the table without him seeing. I don't know why I took it in the first place. Maybe I wanted to get caught. I didn't even want the pipe. I just wanted someone to notice it was missing. All I know is I feel bad stealing from him. I feel bad stealing at all.

We are in the car. Me and the Alcoholic. I tell him where to go, but he doesn't start the car.

"Let's go for a drive, instead."

"I can't. It's work. I have to go to work," I say.

"Nobody works at one in the morning."

"I do. I should."

"We might not see each other again," he says.

"Why's that?"

"I'm leaving school."

"Forever?"

"Maybe."

"Me too," I say.

"What for?" he asks.

"For this," I say.

I look at the clock. It's half past one. It's true. Nobody works this late. Besides, I've been gone so long the "Back in Five" sign is probably yellow with age. All the students lined up to get in have long since gone. Off to bed, to the video store, somewhere. I could tell the scholarship people I had to go to the hospital. I left town on a family emergency. I could tell them I was throwing up blood, got knocked unconscious, had a female problem. I could tell them I was in a room with no clocks. I could tell them sacrifice has no meaning drunk. I could tell them a lot of things.

The Alcoholic pulls out a bottle of wine.

"You wanna learn how to drive a car?" he asks.

"How do you know I can't?"

"I been asking about you," he says and tosses me the keys.

Left side gas, right side brake, or maybe it's the other way around. Everything comes in threes, even him, because I am spinning with cheap Genesee beer. I make the best of it. The car stops and starts with the abruptness of a jump cut. On the next full lurch, he opens his door and dry heaves while we're still moving. This I find unbearably funny, and laugh so hard I don't have time to feel bad, and driving, bad as I am, is glory. I am just glad it's not me dry heaving in front of him.

"We need a corkscrew," he says of the wine. He bites at it, tries pulling it off with his teeth.

"What do you wanna do?" I ask.

There is nothing but houses. All the stores are closed and gas stations are clear across town by now.

"Someone's gotta have one in these houses," he says.

"You're just gonna go in and ask for a corkscrew?"

"I'm not gonna ask."

He tells me to stop the car. He takes the keys out of the ignition, gets out. We stand shivering outside an old Ranch style house. All the lights are out but the porch lights burn, showing us the way. I start up the front steps and he hisses at me.

"What are you doing?"

"Going in," I whisper.

"We're not going to a dinner party," he says. "We're breaking in. You don't break in using the front door."

"Oh," I say, feeling stupid.

I want him to think I've done this before, that I do it all the time. He leads me around the back, pries open a window next to the garage. He weaves his hands together and I step in as he lifts me up and through the window. I fall like wet clay on the other side. I think I am in a laundry room because the smell is Clorox. I look around but can only make out shapeless sweeps of greens and grays. It's too dark in here and I am taken by a claustrophobic terror. I suddenly wonder if he's setting me up. He sticks his head in through the window.

"What are you doing?" he asks.

"Waiting for you," I say.

"Open the door, dummy."

"Oh," I say.

There's a side door next to the garage. I open it. He walks through like a king. "C'mon," he says, crouching down like a green plastic soldier. I assume position behind him as we slug through the swamp. It takes a bit for my eyes to adjust to the light, but when they do I'm seeing with the clarity of night vision. The kitchen is enormous and we open all the drawers until we find a corkscrew. He opens the wine and I open the refrigerator, pull out what's there. I grab a bucket of soggy Kentucky Fried Chicken, strawberry jello mold, American cheese, mayonnaise, bologna, and white bread. The Alcoholic peers his head in.

"Pimento Loaf!" he whispers enthusiastically. I look to see if he's kidding. I grab a leg of chicken, tear off a bite and hand it to the Alcoholic. We continue like that until the entire bucket of chicken is just bones. He hands me the wine and I drink straight from the bottle.

We leave the the dishes on the table, the bottle empty of wine. The Alcoholic has to pee so he props the refrigerator door open, lets the light be our guide. We take off our shoes, go up a flight of stairs. I am wild and delirious with the thrill of it all. But I stay cool, another average day passed busting in and thieving. I follow behind him, assume the appropriate swagger. We pass a room; two people are spooned asleep. Another room is a crib, glow in the dark stars, the light sound of a mobile turning, the faint chimes of Frere Jacques. The hallway stretches out like silly putty before us.

Above, an old ceiling fan turns with laments and moans. I follow him to the end of the hall, where there's a door, but behind it, no bathroom. He covers his lips with a finger, with his other hand he points back down the hall toward the parents' room. We backtrack. We stop on the creaks of the wide wood planks, hold our breath, continue. We stand at the entrance of the master bedroom. My stomach nerves are in my throat.

The mother rolls over. The father follows. They are one unit, a system. Now he spoons her. The Alcoholic creeps in first, nearing the bed to pass. I follow but panic at the foot of the bed frame. I stand like a statue and pray to a working god they remain asleep. The Alcoholic continues, makes his way to the bathroom and disappears for a full minute or so. I crouch down on the floor, comforted and less conspicuous. From the bathroom, I hear the loud stream of piss as he lets go of six plus beers and half a bottle of wine. The sound alone is enough to wake the neighborhood, and it lasts so long I wonder if he'll ever stop. When he's finished, he flushes then gasps at his idiocy. The parents roll over again and I hold my breath. A second or so later, the Alcoholic peers his head out, holds up a roll of toilet paper, and triumphantly lobs it in the air toward me. I panic, but dart to catch it. It hooks on my finger like a horseshoe and I exhale with relief. I turn slowly, like on rivets, and track out of the spooners' room.

On the street outside, he plays Rocky, skipping air rope and jumping jacks. I laugh and watch and then he shadow boxes with me. We go round and round each other, getting closer and closer but keeping our fists up the whole time. When we get back in the car, we scream and laugh and go a bit crazy.

"Pimento Loaf?" I cry.

"What? You don't like your food white trash? Reminds me of home."

I hold up the corkscrew and say,

"Well, then. Here's to home."

He looks me dead in the eye, says,

"Here's to home."

He drives us back to his place. His driving is almost as erratic as mine is, just faster.

The town is a blurry Polaroid with streaks of colored wind, dotted strange with overexposed faces. It's soft around the edges tonight, my body bears no outlines, and the Alcoholic and I have made our first memory together. Maybe one day, I think, I'll tell him about the pipe. I know the school might take my scholarship, but the sacrifice doesn't feel wrong. I would drive out of here into forever with the Alcoholic right now. Maybe school's not the place for a person like me. Perhaps I'm more trouble then I'm worth. It feels good to be this bad, like my world cracked wide open, things fell in, things dropped out. I am a thief, a robber. Maybe one day I'll repent, make amends to people I'll never see again, a town I often hate.

This is our story, how we met. Maybe one day we'll tell it to our kids. That in the course of one night we busted in, stole, lied, and seized what we believed was rightfully ours.

The Alcoholic was taking my heart and I needed something solid to grab onto.

When we get back to the party, people are lying on the couch, watching a documentary about Peg Leg Bates; my weekend friend has long since gone.

"To the hospital," they say.

"Angels were dying at his feet."

I nod like I understand, because in a way I do. I look at the Alcoholic who is starting to look angelic to me. He meets my glance, opens his jacket and lets four rolls of toilet paper fall. We look at it like we have never seen such beauty before. He says he is into Neo-Realism and the French New Wave, but I have a feeling he is more Bogie than Belmondo, because he looks up at me and says,

"You're my only crime, baby."

I don't know what it means, but I like how it sounds, which is pretty much how I feel about all these Fellini films we start renting.

THE SHAPE OF FLORIDA

There's a burn on your back the shape of Florida but you won't tell me how you got it. There have been accidents, ones in cars, ones at home. You have scars from stitches you won't talk about, gashes, and bits of missing skin. You have secrets I want to know. There is stuff you won't talk about, things you deny. If you kept a journal I'd read every page. I want to see through you, memorize your veins. I lick your eyelids when you cry, run my tongue over your lashes. The salt burns on your face but tastes sweet and sad on my tongue. I want to know why people are warning me about you.

You want me to know everything, want to pull out your guts and show me the scars. This is from 1976, you say; this one's from 1981. But when I want to know how, you close up like a border. You were a skate punk as a kid, a speed freak, spent your days flying high on synthetic adrenaline. You were a garage band pioneer. In sixth grade you shaved your head bald, made a mockery out of your junior high class picture. On the field trip to the Vietnam Memorial you cut the words Minor Threat into your forearm. Did it with a piece of old glass you found under the engraved name of a soldier, dead and gone. The punk band is forever immortalized on your skin, raised and pink as a scarrish tattoo, but the reason you did it has long since vanished. Sometimes I wonder if you remember why. Sometimes I wonder if any of us do. You have a burn on your back the shape of Florida and I want to know how you got it.

You point out the other scars. Car accident at fifteen, you say. Go-cart crash at eleven. But you never finger the one on your back, won't tell me a thing about it. I run my hand over it at night when you sleep, try to distinguish its markings. It's reddish tan, like a birthmark, but it's a scar, a burn. It looks unnatural, inorganic. Once I asked you if it hurt when it happened. You looked at me blank, pulled the shirt over your head.

You have dimples, eyes the color of blue star acid, and it's glitter when you smile. You can turn the world upside with your grin. Your teeth are perfect, the color of white-out. You have calluses on your three guitar chord changing fingers. You have a singing voice clear and gorgeous as a wet shiny heart. There are moments I think you'll unfold, roll yourself out like a carpet. Our eyes are shut and we talk late into the night, delicately laying our stories down like paving stones. I don't care that I listen more than talk, that I ask more of you than you do of me.

You have secrets, memories that jar your body awake in jolts. I want to be the chosen one you share it all with. You claim you're busted, come with an out of order sign. You swear I'm your soul mate for now and for always, say I'm the only one that can fix you. I have ego enough to think I can.

You aren't the only one broken.

GRAVITY OF A GRAY WORLD

He is a free therapist. The kind you're assigned, like those lawyers who represent criminals who can't pay. He's like that. His name was picked out of a hat. His ball was spun in a plastic tumbler. It was a lottery. He lost. I won. The Free Therapist is a graduate student at my school, studying for his Ph.D. He's one year in and shows for it. There's a ton of nodding, some sympathetic squinting. He says,

"That must be very painful for you . . . You must be very angry . . . I understand that's very upsetting . . . ."

Sometimes he sounds like the textbooks he studies from; once in a while he looks things up. Occasionally, he gets confused, says,

"Ummm, I don't know how to answer that."

And scribbles a note on a technical looking sheet of Ph.D. paper. These things don't bother me, give me no pause, because the Free Therapist pays attention to me, sees me when I'm speaking. That's what's important.

His office is off-campus and I take the University bus. A bunch of us get off at the same stop. We reach our destination flustered, arching and bending over ourselves. Grabbing at any spare threads of inconspicuousness. The mechanical doors open to the maroon and gray sign announcing what each of us are here for: Psychological Services. The bus sighs, lowers, lets us out single file. A parking lot the length of a city block separates us from the single-story beige building, and we stagger our pace so we're not all walking in unison. Usually I'm the first one to the front door. I speed walk, head down, hands in pockets, drawing out the last inhales of cigarette smoke from the filter. On occasion, I'll hold the door open for everyone, look into their faces as they file past me muttering their thank yous. It's not an act of kindness. I do it because I'm not nice. I say, "Have a good session."

Reminding them they are patients makes them uncomfortable.

Sometimes I hang around afterwards, lean against a car, smoke cigarettes and feel mad. I imagine the Free Therapist watching me after I leave: stealing away to the window, peering out from behind the curtain, pulling it slightly to the side, watching me simmer in all my anger. Sometimes I see him on campus, walking across the lawn with a colleague, a professor. Our eyes never meet, we don't acknowledge the presence of the other, but the hairs on my arms shiver, my chest opens like a drawer when he passes, and I want to fold him up, close him in. I know he sees me; he knows I've seen him, and I love that we share those moments with no one else in the world.

There's not much about me he doesn't know, but there's a cave of him I haven't a clue of. I know which car is his, which days he's off. I know his phone number and the street he lives on. I think about breaking into his house, seeing what's inside, who lives with him. I want to look at the cards and pictures on his mantle, the crayon drawings from his niece on the fridge. I imagine he lives alone, with a couple of cats, a dog, that he is unloved by women and men alike because he is not attractive. I suppose he's unfortunate looking, with the harelip and stumpy eyebrows, but I don't care, I could love him. It's not his face I'm after.

I dream about living with him, me on the pullout couch, him in the bed. In the mornings he cooks me breakfast, readies a brown paper bag with my lunch. We drive to campus together and he kisses my forehead before I leap out of the car. Dinner is on the table when I come home and we eat together like a regular family. Afterwards, while the dishwasher runs, I do my homework at the dining room table while he goes over case files and listens to NPR.

It doesn't occur to me that he has other patients. I'm not a moron; I know the facts of the thing, but I never give it a thought. I am his alone. That's how it feels; that's how it should be. The waiting room doesn't feel like a bus stop. It's always just me waiting for him. On Tuesday I wait for him, flip through *People* magazine. Soon it's five minutes late and I skim *Entertainment Weekly*, the *New Yorker*. Then he's ten, twelve, fifteen, seventeen minutes late and I'm starting to think something happened to him. What if he got hit by a car, knifed by a patient? What if he was shot in a hold-up, walking around with amnesia in the emergency room? How would I know? How would I find out? What would I do if the Free Therapist died? I start alternating between mad and worried. I stagger between the two: ready to blow, call the hospital, throw a fit, check in with reception, make a scene, go to his house. It's twenty minutes late and I am about to get up, go to the front desk, make sure the receptionist intercomed him upon my arrival, when I hear his office door open down the hall. There are two people talking, he and a girl. I hear him say,

"I will see you next week."

And they walk down the hall together toward the waiting room. He stops under the doorframe and I see then, his hand on her shoulder. She is my age, hip, fucked up, in various stages of undress. She looks like a punk, a junky. She looks like me. She turns, gives me a slow steady smirk. As she walks away, she lifts her arm, raises her hand as if to wave, but instead hikes up her middle finger, shoots me the bird, while the rest of her body erases from behind the wall. Her finger stays, lingers on casually for half a second, then disappears into never. The Free Therapist doesn't see any of it, he faces me, smiles, says,

"Come on in."

There are plants, books. The couch I never sit on has a paper towel covering the head pillow. There are two overgrown leather chairs that face each other. He sits on the one near the desk. Behind his chair is a black box tape recorder. All our conversations are chronicled. He plays them for his supervisor; they discuss me anonymously in class. Perhaps they pause, replay parts of conversations, say, "And what could you have done differently here?" I am an experiment, a research project, a test. But I find solace in those tapes, knowing that somewhere in this world together, he and I are immortalized. That we will outlive ourselves. Maybe one day I can listen to them, lull myself to sleep nights to the lift and drop of our conversations.

Sometimes I hate the box, stare at the box when I'm angry. There are moments I want to kick it, rip it open and scratch at the thin magnetic strip. I stare at the box today, but I don't sit down. I pace, making him nervous. I am silent, making him do all the work. My mind is burning itself dry. Several variations of bludgeoning the girl flash in and out, blurry then focused. There are sidewalks, hydrants, mailboxes that I smash her head into repeatedly. That'll show her. Who the hell does she think she is, giving me the finger? Me! Of all people. He cut into my hour by twenty minutes with her and now he owes me. They both owe me. Could it be that he likes her more than me? That he thinks she is more fucked up than I am? Is it possible that in his spare time he thinks about her and not me? Is she going to be his big case, his big break, his dissertation? I am fuming, foaming at the mouth, but I don't talk. I just pace. Back and forth, forth and back until he says,

"Tell me what's on your mind."

"What's on my mind is that you are an asshole," I tell him.

"I see. And what makes me an asshole?"

But I can't say it. As much as I am angry, I don't want to hurt his feelings. I don't want him to think I am jealous of that girl, but I am. I am jealous and threatened and I hate her. I am afraid that if I bring her up, if I talk about her, she'll have all the power, he'll love her more than me.

"Can you tell me? Can you tell me what makes me an asshole?"

"No," I say and plop down on the chair.

"What's going on? What are you thinking about?" he asks.

"You were late," I say.

"Yes, I was. I'm sorry. Does that make you angry?"

"Why were you late?"

"I was with a patient."

"So? That's never made you late before."

"No, it hasn't. I apologize and I hope it doesn't happen again."

I stand up, offended.

"That's it? That's all you have to say on the matter? That's fucking bullshit. You're bullshit."

I walk over to the window, peek out from behind the opening in the curtains. The parking lot is gray, filled with gray cars under a gray sky in a gray city in a gray world, and there leaning against a gray Saab, is the girl, the middle finger girl, exhaling gray smoke and waiting for her gray life to fill black with remorse and resign. Before this place, this bad age of twenty, my life was wide, unlike the sky here, closed in on itself like me when mad. I turn before she can see me. I turn and face him, the Free Therapist, and say,

"You're nothing."

"I'm nothing what?" he asks.

"That's it," I say. "You're just nothing. We're all nothing."

But I don't think he's nothing at all. He's the whole universe. He is the one that can save me. I am waiting for him to grab me by the scruff of my neck, toss me into his life like a stray.

"Do you think you are nothing?"

"I know I'm nothing," I say.

"And what makes you know that?" he asks.

"I am not important."

"Important to whom?" he asks.

"To anyone."

"You think you're not important to me?"

"I know I'm not."

"How do you know?"

I want to tell him why, that he was late, that he was twenty minutes late because of her, but I can't. I feel foolish for this. I feel as if he has betrayed me, cheated on me by having another patient, by having another me as a patient. I thought I was the only me he had, but I was wrong. There are more of me, and perhaps even more than I think. I thought I was special, unique. But I feel like a type, a mold. I am just another shape for a cookie cutter. A Christmas tree, a horseshoe, a dog.

I wonder why I've never seen her before, if she's a transfer student. I wonder what her name is, what her problem is. I wonder if she's cooler than I am, more fucked up, tougher than me, stronger. I wonder if she lives in a dorm or off-campus. I wonder if she is as bullshit as I think she is. She is nothing, a plastic disposable key chain.

I sit back down in the chair and stare at him. He looks at me expectantly, as if I am going to tell him the very thing he wants to hear. But I decide not to say a word. If I am not enough for him, if he needs another girl like me, then I'm not telling him another thing. My life is private. My feelings are for me. He can go to hell.

"Why do you think you're not important to me?" he asks tenderly, sweetly and it makes me want to take it all back, rewind and record over all my words.

"I don't know."

"Ahhh, what's our rule? There are no 'I don't knows' in here."

"You were late."

"And that makes you angry."

"Yes."

"That makes you feel like you're not important."

"Yes."

"How can I make it up to you? How can I let you know that you are important to me?"

"I don't know," I say. But I do know.

"What's the rule?"

I smile against my better judgment.

"Are you jealous of that girl?"

"No!" I defend too fast.

"Are you sure?"

"Yes, I'm sure," I say. I take a studied pause before I ask what I really want to know,

"What's her problem anyway?"

"You know I can't tell you that."

"Tell me anyway. Does she have dumb boy problems, or is she like, a junky?"

"Do you think boy problems are dumb?"

"Yeah."

"Do you have boy problems?"

"No."

"Are you a junky?"

"No."

"So, then, let's talk about you. Why don't we leave her business alone?"

But I couldn't leave her business alone.

I don't intend to follow her, it just happens. It always seems that once you don't want to run into someone, they're everywhere. I see her in the cafeteria, the Student Union, the University Bookstore. She is always alone; she never looks up. I don't have a solid plan, I just want to scare her, let her know she screwed with the wrong girl. I'm going to give her more than the finger.

I trail her to a lecture on string theory one Saturday afternoon and watch her as she sits in the back row, eyes closed, smiling, nodding through the whole thing. I think she is riding a fix, lying back after chasing the dragon, but when the lecture is over, she claps and stands, and I can tell from her expression, the urgency behind her eyes, that she is present and conscious, and understood it all, from quarks to quantum mechanics.

She speeds across the winding cobblestone path, arms wrapped around her chest like a straitjacket. Her Bauhaus tee shirt is vintage, ten or so years old and ripped, held together by safety pins. Her skirt is too long, twigs and leaves become ensnarled in the tassels and a mini forest drags behind her like a bridal train as she walks. She is gothic punk, but her bad taste splays on her like psoriasis. A belt with thick silver studs hangs as an ornament low on her waist. She stops to light a cigarette, turns her body forty-five degrees away from the wind.

I follow her all the way down to the lake, into the woods. She pauses at the lake, grabs at the gravel on the ground and tosses pebbles, disrupting the sleeping lake. She is good at skipping them. One hops and skims almost the entire length of the lake. I consider pushing her in.

In the woods she sits on a rock, bends over her bag real low. She pulls something out, then something else. I figure she's gonna tie off a vein, shoot up, cook some heroin in a burnt spoon in these woods, but she stays hunched over, still as wax, giving a blessing, saying a prayer. White patches of breath rise above her head. She sits up from time to time, takes a drag off a cigarette, looks around. I duck down real low behind a tree and feel somewhat like a pervert. She bends down again, begins rocking back and forth, side to side like a cradle. Smoke loops up and behind her, sucked off to heaven with the wind.

I imagine throwing rocks at her, pulling out a switchblade, showing her what I'm made of, but I don't have a knife and the only rocks around are pebbles. I stay crouched, waiting for the right moment to pounce. Soon she hikes up her skirt and I see dark stains the size and shape of eyeballs tracked down the length of her leg. I think, what the hell are those? But then I see. She is burning herself up, scarring stories into her skin with the cherry of her cigarette. I am caught in the moment of not wanting to be there and not wanting to leave.

Each wound is deliberate, plotted. She holds the burnt end of the cigarette to her skin, closes her eyes while it lances, cringes until she can't bear any more. Each time though, she holds out a little longer, endures a little more pain. She takes a drag, burns a hole, takes a drag, burns a hole. Guilt expands in me like the gritty sound from a white noise machine and I close my eyes, trying to erase it, erase her.

I don't know how many cigarettes she goes through that day, or what else she brings out of her bag, but I feel sad for her because I understand this, what she's doing. Before she can see me, I turn and leave, staying low and slow, taking the edge off the crunch of leaves. I trail through campus the long way. There are initials carved into trees, cigarette filters driven into the earth and I think, we're not so different from the bark, so different from the dirt.

There is a film on me then and for a few days after. Something like a coating I feel but can't see. It's as if I read about myself in someone else's journal, witnessed something that wasn't mine to see, like another couple having sex, my father getting out of the shower, my roommate masturbating. It's funny how sometimes you think you want to know something about a girl, but it's not that girl you learn about.

STATE OF EMERGENCY

I've been holding in my piss for the better part of an hour, but the Alcoholic doesn't like to stop unless forced, so I curse him out, and we pull off Exit 15. The mini mall is closed, the gas station chained. He throws an empty bottle of Snapple at me and says, "Crouch." I sit on it and fill it back up.

They say it's a state of emergency, because the State of New York is bleached white. The blizzard has been three days long. The trees turned to ice statues and the city closed around us like a salt shaker. First semester finals are over and we drive seven hours to a canceled party in Brooklyn. By the time we make it, the roads have closed from Canada to New York City. We decide to call it a long weekend and crash at my mother's in the West Village.

The first night the Alcoholic and I station ourselves in the living room to look at old photo albums. My mother sees to it that the Alcoholic not handle the pictures directly and that his wrestling sneakers are parked in the frozen foyer three rooms from the new Persian rug. She surveys the Alcoholic from the doorway as he flips the stiff cardboard pages. She fake-smiles whenever he turns her way.

The Alcoholic and I get drunk off stolen bags of wine from WorldWide News where he works the Lotto stand on weekends. My mom drinks a bottle of vintage red imported from France and gets loaded the way rich people do: in style. He tells her he wants to start a revolution and she tells him that seems appropriate. Before passing out he asks me how he did with her and I say,

"Just fine."

He beams and says,

"Yeah, she ate me up."

I feel bad for him and fall asleep.

I am on my third college in two years. My transcript has me as a sophomore but I am three years in. The Alcoholic is a senior fixed on writing a thesis. The search for a topic is becoming more the project than the actual project itself. He can't keep an idea down; one after another heaves out of him like food poisoning. The ideas themselves are bile: Nazi Propaganda Films, Lost Nazi Propaganda Footage, and finally, Found Nazi Propaganda Outtakes. When he discovers five other History students are going the Nazi Propaganda route, he sniffs cliché and resurrects The Populist Revolution—a concept he lifts from a conversation overheard in the library stacks.

He gets work at the news kiosk, WorldWide, starts talking about the working class and begins carrying around a couple of hot titles: *Kill Your Parents Before They Kill You: An Illustrated Manifesto for Surviving the 90s and Before*; *The Populist Moment: A Short History of the Agrarian Revolt in America*, and *There's Nothing in the Middle of the Road but Yellow Stripes and Dead Armadillos*. He ends up with just one favorite sticking out of his back pocket: *Sam Smith's Great American Political Repair Manual: How to Rebuild Our Country So the Politics Aren't Broken and Politicians Aren't Fixed*. He wants to start a revolution for ordinary people, to lead the blue-collar masses in a progressive movement toward empowerment. Perhaps when the revolution starts, I'll sign up, but for now I just want to graduate in one year and make a movie.

The weekend is a bust and we spend it in bed until even that's a bore. My mother hasn't counted on our long stay and she plants her silent protests strategically. To the left of the refrigerator she has placed a tip jar. When we return upstairs from a downstairs jaunt, our bed has been stripped of sheets, our suitcases placed open on the floor. She handles our dirty clothes as carefully as a dirty bomb, tossing them into a hefty bag, fixing post-its asking, "garbage?" I find it amusing that after each encounter with the Alcoholic she goes to the bathroom to wash her hands, and he goes to the kitchen to pull off another round on her scotch.

The air goes sour and staying at my mom's is starting to stink. With a day left there is nothing to do except drive back, but the streets are closed and people are warned about dying. My mom turns the dial when weather warnings are issued; she changes the station on radio broadcasts interrupted by storm alerts. She gives hourly reports on the road's condition by peering out the window. "It doesn't look so bad anymore . . . You're fine to drive back . . . The earlier you leave the better . . . I don't want you driving in the dark, God forbid you hit an animal."

The radio says you can't drive anywhere, but the Alcoholic wants out and all my mom's scotch is dried up. He wants to get back to the kiosk where he belongs. He is, after all, working-class America. He says the big city is contaminating him. Manhattan is nothing but a let-down. He thinks maybe after all is said and done he should live on a prairie, be a farmer, raise cattle, milk a cow. This town is arctic, but he is on fire. I don't know how to drive so that lands me a passenger, even in decisions. He says, let's hit it, and we do.

The car is parked in an outdoor lot off the highway. The attendants moved it to the top level overlooking the Hudson, but they won't drive it down. The hill up is iced like a rink and we slip backwards every few steps. We are out of breath by the time we reach the top. The Alcoholic is anemic and sweating. He has to sit down for a minute. I find the trowel in the backseat, but he won't let me stay in the car until he's done scraping the ice from the windshield. I do my bit and take one swipe at a window with my glove. The snow falls to the ground like a haircut.

It takes seven minutes before the car will start.

We slide downhill despite pressing the pedals. At the bottom he starts laughing from the thrill of it. My nervous habits kick in—biting my nails, twirling my hair, picking at scabs. I think we should get out and go home. We can hold out a day or two; school will be shut down anyway. Upstate will be ten times worse than the city. Besides we can stay in bed and have sex for a couple more days. We count bills, but don't have enough for a hotel. When I refuse to sleep in the car, he looks at me smooth and presses on forward.

The West Side Highway is dead as a corpse. The piers stick out like white caskets over the mouth of the Hudson. The dog-walkers, prostitutes, joggers, and bikers are all on-call till summer. Across the river, New Jersey sits still as a waistband. A boat is forgotten on the Hudson, like a ducky in a baby's bath. We think we'll run green lights the whole way, but the time it takes from one light to the next is a crawl, and we stop and salute each red glowing circle as cautious as visitors from out of town. The car wants to go sideways, but the Alcoholic says he knows tricks for straightening things out. When the front of the car veers to the right, he pulls it to the left. When the front of the car veers left, he pulls it to the right. We slide like that for a good while up the West Side Highway. A man wrapped tight for shipping walks 12th Avenue at a quick clip. His pace is faster than ours is and I point him out to the Alcoholic who says,

"The walk of shame."

"You think?"

"Oh please. I could pick that walk out of a lineup."

"That's reassuring."

He lets out an over-dramatic sigh, but doesn't meet my glance.

The Highway's stretch is infinity and we are calculating our way.

We are either the sole survivors after apocalypse, or the stupidest people on Earth, I argue. The radio is dead; the tapes are all frozen, so he sings me Nirvana songs and we creep along like geriatrics. He fiddles with the heater, keeping one hand on the wheel and the other on the little knob. I tell him to keep his eyes on the road. He argues there is nothing to keep his eyes on, we are the only ones for miles. I put his hand back on the steering wheel, and take over the heat. It's futile, the only air we get is cold, and when the last of the heat ducks out, we are drowned in frost. We fight over the sleeping bag and skid clear across the fast lane. We could have stopped short right there and no one would ever know. We haven't passed another car on this trip, isn't that a bit strange?

"It's a state of emergency," he says.

"I know."

"That means you're not allowed to drive, dumbass."

"Seriously?"

"Quite."

When you don't drive, as I don't, you tend not to know things, even the most mundane and pedantic of things, such as this thing, this no-driving-rule-filed-under-S for State of Emergency.

"Could we get into trouble?"

"Only if we're pulled over."

"And what would happen?"

"Jail," he says, smiling like he can't wait.

He is thrilled with himself, as if this mission is daring in some heroic way. As if he is saving lives instead of risking them. I unwrap another pack of Camel Lights and light two. I put one in his mouth and we smoke like thugs. His hands are at ten after nine on the wheel. His fingernails are outlined in dirt. The cuticles are torn up; there is dried blood around his pinky. He lifts his left hand, uses his thumb to crack the knuckle on his index finger. It pops and he rests it back on the wheel. The snow starts to come down as sleet, but he doesn't put the wipers on. He presses his face up close to the glass, drives like an old man reading the paper at his nose.

The sun is in another country. The hail beats down on both sides of the car. The slick sound of highway slaps under our wheels. The air smells of wet clay. The Alcoholic gets silent, the way a teakettle does right before the hiss. After five months of being together daily I am getting familiar with his patterns. I know he is a car crier and a night talker. He glances out the side window, puckers his lips. His eyes start to tear, a couple fall spotting his black jeans. I scoot closer, catch one on my fingertip as it rolls toward his mouth.

"Can I have this?"

He smiles.

"What are you thinking about?" I ask quietly.

He shakes his head like he doesn't want to talk about it, but I know he does. He likes when it feels like pulling teeth.

"What is it, monster? You can tell me."

He wipes his eyes quick and rough with the sleeve of pea coat.

"Hey, careful with those eyes. They're half mine," I say.

He smiles.

"I'm so lucky to have you," he tells me. I smile and put my arm around him.

"You take such good care of me," he says.

I let that hang there for a second.

"Do you think I'm gonna be a bum? Like for real? Like homeless and unemployed?" he asks.

"No. Why do you say that?" I ask.

"That's what everyone says."

"Who's everyone?" I ask.

"My mom, my dad . . . Moe."

Moe is the ex-girlfriend and my stomach turns every time she is mentioned. She is anorexic, alcoholic, and trouble is rusted to her chrome interior. She is beautiful and although I don't know her, his friends do. She is a year or two older, a Religion major who writes poetry in black textured sketchbooks she binds with dirty rubber bands. Her hair is dark blonde, wavy, long. Her face is beautiful, small with perfect, small features, a scattering of light red freckles across and around the bridge of her small Anglo nose. She wears white flowy poet shirts, big floppy hats. And although I know these details and silently harp on them from time to time, it is the unfortunate information that makes doing so worthwhile. She has a thick neck, is a social misfit, and doesn't have one female friend. But it is her name that makes me smile. It is Moe for short. Short for Maureen. Calling her Maureen out loud makes the Alcoholic cringe. I use it sparingly for effect, but I use it.

Maureen dumped the Alcoholic. Left him outside of Breugger's Bagels after Sunday brunch. Poor guy even paid. Outside on the street when he took her hand, she pulled away, said, "Don't." Said she was uncomfortable holding hands with her ex-boyfriend and then, she walked away. Left him. Never returned his phone calls, didn't answer his letters, nothing. Maureen was done. She went on a bender, set her house on fire, and now lives somewhere on the West Coast under the care and supervision of egg-shaped nurses in an exclusive rehab resort.

"They all think I'm gonna be a failure. My teachers, my old bosses, everyone. Everyone thinks I'm a waste. Even my mom thinks I'm gonna be a bum. Everyone in my life but you believes that."

"They don't know what they're talking about."

"Would you love me if I were homeless?" he asks.

"You're not gonna be homeless."

"What if my legs had to be amputated. Would you love me if I had no legs?" he asks.

"How did you lose your legs?"

"Farming accident."

"Dangerous profession, that."

"What about my arms, what if I had no arms. Would you love me then?"

"Farming accident?"

"No, skiing."

"You're homeless with lift tickets—not a bad gig."

"Okay, not skiing, um . . . mining."

"Mining? Where the fuck are you living?"

"Tennessee."

"Tennessee? You want to live in Tennessee?"

"Well, wherever. I'm in a mining accident and I lose my arms and my legs . . ."

"I thought the legs went in a farming accident."

"No, I step on a land mine and they all blow off. Would you love me then?"

I go quiet picturing my boyfriend, the torso.

"What if I were just a head?" he asks.

The image is precious and I buckle with laughter, my body forgetting the cold, heating itself naturally. He laughs too, laughs and swerves and I pull myself together enough to say, "Keep your eyes on the road."

My hands aren't warming up, and his are starting to shake. He is ravenous and all the fast food is shut down, so we pull off Exit 171 to search for food off the highway. We scout the town twice before we spot her. She is five, maybe six. She is standing outside her house knocking, yelling, but no one is letting her in. Her gold hair has icicles and she is wearing nothing under her cotton nighty. We are so gone we think we're dreaming her, but I run out of the car and snatch her up. She could be made from twigs and branches. I could carry her for miles. I think she'll scream when I pick her up, but she wraps her arms and legs tight around me; she holds on to me like a backpack.

In the car I swaddle her in my sleeping bag coat, tell her we'll get her somewhere warm. I gently untangle the small chunks of ice from her hair. I brush the crusted snow from her nightgown. The bottom is lined with embroidered flowers. Her toenails are painted pink. She is stiff with winter; she would trust anyone. Her name is Megan; she has a lisp. She had gone outside for snowballs and snow angels, but her parents, still sleeping, hadn't heard the knocking. I figure she's been out nearly a half an hour. Her toes start to hurt warming up, and she moans and weeps in my arms until she finds her thumb. She is quiet as we drive around trying to figure out what to do with her. The Alcoholic is too hungry to think. Megan closes her eyes and starts to drift. The Alcoholic freaks, tells me to wake her, that if she falls asleep she'll die. I don't understand the logic, but I jolt her and she opens her eyes and cries.

I don't know how we missed Darlene's Muffins the first time around because it is practically right there, the first store in the town of Deposit. The Alcoholic knocks and knocks and I stay in the car rubbing Megan's baby feet, jarring her awake whenever her eyes close. Darlene answers the door, annoyed. Her stomach falls in rolls over her elastic sweat pants and her gray short hair is so thinned on top you can see the crown of her scalp. The Alcoholic talks and points toward us with the urgency of a silent movie star. Darlene bends down to see Megan and nods her head. A second wind rushes us when the Alcoholic opens the car door on my side. He looks at us and I hand

Megan to him, but instead of taking her he backs away and says,

"It's cool. Bring her in."

I lift her, one arm underneath her neck, the other underneath her knees. She lies across me like a tragic heroine saved from a fire. The Alcoholic is afraid of her and that pisses me off. Inside, Darlene turns on all the lights, and the store is Mom-and-Pop from counter to ceiling. Megan knows her phone number by heart, and after calling her parents, Darlene makes us instant oatmeal and heats some muffins. She props Megan in front of a TV in the back room, and the three of us sit at a table looking at each other for answers.

"It's a state of emergency out there," Darlene accuses us.

"Yeah, we know," the Alcoholic says.

"You shouldn't be driving. Cops already arrested someone up there in Utica."

The toaster dings and I look at the Alcoholic with I-told-you-so-eyes. Darlene cuts the muffin tops and lets a wedge of butter melt into each section before putting them back in the toaster oven. She stands over us fiddling with her cross necklace like counting rosaries.

"You students?"

We nod. We are starving, and the smell of the burning butter is making saliva.

"You up at Ithaca?"

"Near."

The toaster sounds again and she sets out the muffins before us. We grab them up and vacuum them in. One is not enough and she heats up another round of butter-baked corn muffins. Megan putters in, warm and hungry. Her parents don't live so far, what is taking them so long? I start to fantasize about keeping her. She can live with me, my roommate. She'll sleep in my bed, on the left side. I'll clear a couple drawers in the bureau for her things. I'll send her to day care or some sort of community-based program while I attend classes, but we'll always eat breakfast and dinner together. I might call her Maggie instead of Megan, maybe even Maisie; we can change it legally if she wants. Her friends will sleep over. I'll make her a key of her own so she'll never be locked out and near-freeze to death again.

Her little cheeks are flushed and her ears turn burnt umber as they thaw. She smiles up at me, her sweet little legs swing back and forth against her chair. I want her. The rapping on the door startles us and Darlene lets out a shriek deep and quick as a puncture wound—Megan's parents.

The father's face is covered in hair and his hunting cap is dried with blood. His canvas coveralls are pulled high under a Carhartt jacket and his pants are tucked in to Timberlands. The mother is a little mess of a woman. Rail thin, with wild drunken eyes; her bathrobe hangs out of her down coat. The red scarf hangs around her neck, bored, useless. I wait for her to rush to Megan. To pick her up, hug her, give the obligatory gushing thanks to the two young heroes. But she just stands there shivering; one hand clings to her husband's coat pocket, the other wipes the shiny varnish from her nose. Megan continues eating her muffin, barely able to pry her mouth off the porous velvet middle. The silence is unsettling. They aren't much for small talk, I guess.

"Don't eat all the woman's food," the mom says.

"It's okay," Darlene responds.

"I hope she wasn't too big a pain in the ass," the mom says.

"She was fine," I say. "A real trooper."

Darlene pours more sugar in her Sanka; the Alcoholic fills his cup back up.

The father is staring at something over his shoulder, a thermostat. He turns his whole attention to it, fiddles with it. The mother's red scarf is sliding down her coat toward the floor. No one says a word as it falls to a heap on the ground.

"Below zero out there," he says.

"Well, hurry up now. You took up enough of these nice people's time," her mother snaps.

Megan puts the muffin down and slides off the stool. Her lips are the color of faded denim. Her bare feet, ashen. She walks to her mother, takes her hand but looks at me. Her eyes are adult, already set in their ways, and I know out of that family of three, she is the loneliest. I can see them now, walking down the streets of Deposit, the mother half a block ahead of her child, never turning to see if she fell, was abducted. It is a family that doesn't look back, that doesn't double check. The father opens the front door and walks out.

The motor of his truck starts and within seconds the most sound to come out of that man is that of relentless honking. Megan picks up the red scarf, holds it out to her mother. The mother takes it, bunches it up, shoves it in her coat pocket. The girl opens the door for her mother and they leave one after the other. The mother in her down coat, the daughter in her nightgown.

The Alcoholic and Darlene continue eating. Somehow I have found myself standing. Closer to the door than I was before. Nearer to Megan than I perhaps realized.

"Seem like nice folks," Darlene says, as she gets up to clear the table.

"Yeah," the Alcoholic agrees.

It takes us fifteen minutes before we can start the car. Our hands numb up again and the car feels stiff and inflexible like arthritic legs. We pull away from Darlene's and get back on the Highway. We take the fast lane this time; the road is still ours.

It is getting darker. We don't talk the entire sundown. I can't even meet his glance, but I feel him looking at me from time to time, and it's pissing me off.

"Are you mad at me?" he asks finally, his voice whiney, defeated.

"Why'd you say her parents were nice?"

"I don't know."

"Did you think they were nice?"

"They were okay."

"No, they weren't. They weren't even worried about her."

"You don't know their story."

"I don't need to," I say.

"People do crazy things in a state of emergency," he says.

The road ahead is curved steel gray and every town we pass looks the same to me. Why did the Alcoholic say her parents were nice? They weren't nice. They were hateful, selfish. If we hadn't found her, would they have known she was missing? Their own kid was exposed, unwrapped, but they kept their jackets on, put scarves in their pockets. Megan was frozen, frozen to her bones.

The sky is dairy cream and we skid on the surface of her reflection. I turn around, watch the road get smaller. It shrivels until it finally disappears behind me, but maybe it's me that's shrinking. There are no houses anymore, just barns, just highway. The farther we get from Manhattan, the lonelier I feel.

THE END OF THE WORLD

The Alcoholic and I are here for the band we follow, and the drugs. The Atomic Hogs are alternative and even though people say they're losing their edge, we don't mind. We met the drummer in a bar in Montreal, so we'll feel pretty important in the crowd. The four winds arrive at the end of the world the same time every year, give or take an hour, maybe a day. This year, it's on Earth Day, and we are determined to get there. The drive is a nightmare, but we heard it's a sin to miss it and if anything, that was true. The end of the world used to be a burial ground, but now it's a college. The Alcoholic says,

"Same difference."

They call it the end of the world because the field drops like a cliff. People plunge off like accidental skydivers. The plummet takes someone every year, and legend goes it's where the four winds meet. Get caught in the nexus; you'll go crazy for sure. A phenomenon, really. Nature working her last nerve. Some people think it heals; some think it harms. The Alcoholic says,

"We'll be the judge of that."

The Alcoholic and I have decided to hallucinate annually, as part of our own private Earth Day celebration. It's an art school so we know the drugs will be extra potent.

"Poets wouldn't tolerate skunk weed," I tell him.

"Painters neither," the Alcoholic argues.

We are in good hands.

There are only five hundred students, and I wonder if they knew they'd be living on top of dead people. They call it the end of the world, so that's what we call it, too. Mad minds meet there. Kids die. Students go insane. But it's where the parties are. I don't have designs to get stuck at the end of the world, but the Alcoholic does. He packed the camera. They say the school is the most expensive in the country, its students the richest. The road onto campus stretches a mile and the old joke goes, why do the students here feel so at home? Because the driveway's so goddamn long.

The dorms are converted horse stables. Colonial style clapboard barns are arranged around a common lawn, six on each side. The quaintness is deceptive at first. The green wooden shutters, the small white hutches. The place smells like primer and everyone has on carpenter pants, tee shirts with stains. We fit in with no real creases, but the place is so goddamn small we are discovered ten minutes in by a kid named Wexler. He's got dred locks from dirty hair, and when we meet him he's combing out a knot the size of a hand grenade. He takes us to his room, shows us his bicycle bong. It's a two-person deal—one pedals while the other one lights and inhales. The peddler does all the real work; there's none of that exhaling out before sucking in crap. He has a refrigerator filled with liquid acid and he offers us a dropper. We just want mushrooms and a good view of the Atomic Hogs. He walks us across the hall.

This guy Sebby has Fugazi blasting on his portable. A cheese knife is stuck in the back of his door. A baseball bat embedded with nails hangs from the ceiling. We walk in on him shooting metal pellets from a BB gun out the window at his ex-girlfriend's head. He misses. He offers us a turn; we decline. Sebby is fresh out of stock, which is a good thing considering. Wexler walks us across the lawn to Booth House. He leads with his feet like his upper body is being pulled back by a string. I walk behind him and watch. The disentangled dred lock sticks out from the side of his head like a pinecone. He wants to know what we came for, and before I can say Atomic Hogs, the Alcoholic says,

"The end of the world, man."

Wexler stops, smiles. He turns his back on us, points down the long, narrow field.

"There she is," he says. "That's the end of the world."

From where we stand it looks like the horizon drops off, but Wexler assures us it doesn't. He says there's an optical illusion, but you can't be certain until you are at the edge.

"You want to see it?" he asks.

The walk down is peaceful. Mountains surround the campus. Trees guard the end of the world on both sides like the Secret Service. This is a meadow really, a place to bring picnics and boyfriends and families. I wonder if there are ever campfires at the end of the world. You would think that for such a big event, people would be down there already, waiting for the four winds to meet, but it's empty. Everyone is farther up, near the main house that overlooks the common lawn. The students are smoking and drinking and lying around, but they are at a distance. A safe distance, I think. The walk is a good ten minutes and we pass all the dorms until trees take their place. When we get to the edge I look over and see that you can't fall off, but you can roll down. A slope, a wide sledding hill of sorts, but not a cliff. We turn around to look at the main house which looks like a molar, small and jagged.

"It's not so scary down here," I say to Wexler.

"Not now," Wexler says. "Nothing's scary when the sun's out."

We walk back toward the main campus to Booth House and meet Stash. He's pacing back and forth in the common room like he's been waiting for us. His feet are colossal, maybe a size twelve or thirteen, and I wonder how he ever found steel-tip boots in his size. A dead possum nailed to a cross hangs on the wall. A television monitor paused on a pornographic cum shot gives off the low hiss of feedback. They had thrown a party the night before—the "Trailer Trash Sex" party. Things happened, people got hurt, and everyone in Booth House is going to college court. That is, after the weekend. Today however, the Atomic Hogs are playing, the four winds are meeting, and we are in the middle of a drug deal.

Stash's room is wallpapered in tin foil. Even his ceiling. He says it makes him feel like he's back in the womb. I feel like we're inside a cheap condom wrapper. An urgent draft floods his room and I look up to jagged edges of a broken windowpane. The remains grind under our feet and a tingling shoots down my jaw from the sound. On his bed, an army-green duffel bag houses hundreds of clear plastic bags, assorted paraphernalia, and a motley supply of drugs. He sits down next to it, starts pulling out gear. There are grinders, razors, mirrors, burnt spoons, glass vials, strainers, small plastic tubes, used syringes, rolling papers, alligator clips, black balls of tar, red pills, blue pills, yellow pills, oddly shaped pieces of folded brown paper, small bricks of plaited tin foil, and blotter acid. He tosses us a dime bag of aged and dried up pot.

"These aren't mushrooms," I say.

"Oh. Yeah. I don't have mushrooms."

I roll my eyes at him and the Alcoholic squeezes my hand, like everything will be okay. Stash says a group of them are going to drop Wexler's liquid acid in a room downstairs. If we want we can join them, smoke the pot, see the band, walk to the end of the world.

The room downstairs is dark, clammy. There are two metal-framed army cots with clothes piled high on top of them. On the floor: Converse high-top sneakers spray painted gold, tattoo needles, and a pile of vintage record albums. A bunch of young art students are lying on top of each other and when the Alcoholic and I walk in they perk up. New life is desperately needed in this place.

It's cold even though it's April and people are layered in sweaters, jackets. Nick Drake is playing on the turntable. People are burning out cigarettes on the floor. I notice a girl sleeping on one of the beds. No one seems to pay attention to her when she rolls over, groans. She wants us out, I can tell, and when I pull on the Alcoholic's hand and motion to the bed, a girl on the floor says in a fake English accent,

"Don't worry about her."

"What's she got?" I ask.

No one answers.

The girl with the fake English accent is part Asian, part something else. She wears bright red bridge-and-tunnel lipstick, big gold hoop earrings, her hair is thickly gelled, slicked back and pulled up in a high pony tail. Her name hangs on a gold plate around her neck. She pulls at the frayed edges of the gauze bandage that is loosely wound around her right hand. Even though it is freezing out she wears just a tank top and I notice a design razored into her upper arm. It's the anarchy symbol and the scab has been picked enough that a scar is taking its shape. She catches me looking and asks,

"Do you want one?"

I shake my head no.

"What are you here for?" she asks.

"The Atomic Hogs," I answer.

"You're sort of early, don't you think?"

I shrug. The Alcoholic is pretty quiet. I think he feels as in over his head as I do. He's playing it tough as he reaches for the bottle of whiskey and asks,

"May I?"

A few minutes later the Alcoholic is warm too and he sits down with the others. It's just me that's left standing. Wexler climbs in through the window, behind him is a dwarf, or a little person, or

"Kneel," as they call him. I think this is incredibly mean until I find out later his name is actually Neil, and his parents just never put it together. Wexler tosses a backpack on the ground. In it, twenty Visine-sized bottles of liquid acid. Fake English Accent inspects them, looks at Wexler.

"What are they cut with?"

"Forty proof," he answers.

"You're a good man, Wex."

Fake English Accent props the knapsack on her lap, looks at me directly and asks,

"Who's first?"

"We just want mushrooms," I say.

"Mushrooms? What're you guys, a bunch of heads?" she accuses us. The Alcoholic looks up.

"Heads? What's that, like a hippie?" he asks.

"Yeah," she says. "You a coupla hippies?"

"No," says the Alcoholic. "We just know what we want."

"Funny," she says, looking him dead in the eye. "So do I."

A kid on the floor says,

"Better put a leash on your boyfriend."

After a minute of thinking, I say,

"I don't own him."

Everyone is quiet. The Alcoholic looks down, nervous. His hands are in his pockets. The record plays track three, "Road," and it skips, stuck in a groove, caught on a scratch it can't cross. Throats clear. Knuckles crack. People breathe. Fake English Accent's eyes are the darkest I've ever seen, an inaccessible black. I don't look away. I am trying to prove I am just as impermeable. The affect is that I will kick her ass if I have to, but my hope is she's not telepathic. She scares the hell out of me and I want to get out of this room, maybe go home.

Someone turns off Nick Drake, puts on Joe Walsh. Fake English Accent looks around the room, points to a girl in all black.

"Sarah. You're first."

Sarah gives her a generous and appreciative smile.

"Thanks," she gushes, as if being picked first to drop acid is approval, a secret code shared just between them. She thinks she's been chosen as the new best friend, but if anything, it's the other way around. Sarah scoots over to Fake English Accent, lays her head on her lap and stares up at her, waiting.

"How many drops?" Fake English Accent asks.

"Four," Sarah responds.

Fake English Accent opens a dropper bottle, holds open the lid of Sarah's left eye and drops in six hits.

"NEXT!" Fake English Accent yells.

The Alcoholic and I watch the whole sequence. Fake English Accent administers the acid into everyone's eyes and then Wexler administers them into hers. She goes for four in each eye. We are the only ones left. The Alcoholic looks at me.

"You wanna do it?" he asks.

"I wanna do mushrooms," I say.

"But no one has them," he answers.

"I don't know. It seems kinda freaky. I'm not a big eyeball person."

"We'll do it together. It'll be okay. I'll be with you."

Fake English Accent looks at us.

"Don't be such little girls. What kind of pussy-assed school do you go to that you've never eye-dropped before?"

We don't say anything. The Alcoholic slides over to Fake English Accent, lays his head on her lap, looks her in the eyes and says,

"Four drops."

It takes a while, but they finally convince me, using methods only fourteen-year-olds fall prey to. They guilt me, mock me, cajole me, isolate me, attack me. I do two in each eye and after thirty minutes, no one feels a thing. We get two more drops. Forty-five minutes and we are hyper, not hallucinating. Wexler lets us finish off the bottles. We put them on our tongues this time. It hits us hard in fifteen minutes.

We are in another house. Dewey. We are in Dewey. We are in the room with all the lights on. Music is blasting, and we keep playing the same song over and over again. I don't know what it is, but it's catchy and I know all the words the second time around. We are hot as hell and somehow we wind up in other people's clothes. The Alcoholic and I fill a bath and get in, boots and all. Someone comes in with a video camera and then somebody else comes in and gives us gum.

We have someone dim the lights because the brightness is starting to burn our eyes out. Someone sets fire to a chair. Someone else puts it out. There is shrieking, laughing, pawing, spinning, grinding. There are light trails. Impressions of foot and handprints glow in the air. The Alcoholic and I look in the mirror and see how ugly we are. Our hands and face are the color of wet flour. It's still early, only five or so, and the Atomic Hogs aren't playing until nine. The four winds aren't meeting until eleven. We have time and I want to use it.

Outside the trees stand in a circle around us. We lie down and the branches are arms, hands. The grass looks artificial, like fluorescent AstroTurf. I skim my hand over its surface. I can feel each blade individually; they are soft but sharp, like eyelashes. The trees reach down, gesticulating wildly in the wind. We lie on the lawn until the grass hairs make us itch and we think the bugs from the soil are settling into our skin. It freaks me out and I stand up and go back inside. Wexler is riding his bike down the stairs. People are drawing on the walls, spray-painting the ceiling, the floor, putting lit matches to the upholstery.

Fake English Accent and some guy are dry humping on the couch.

I go upstairs to find the Alcoholic. I go into Sebby's room by accident. He is jacking off and I turn quickly and flee as he says,

"No. Wait."

In Wexler's room a pimply kid in Euro get-up—oversized blazer, baggy black pants with pleats, John Lennon glasses—sits on the bicycle bong reading Proust. Stash is in the hall giving someone a piggyback and when he sees me he winks. I smile, but get the creep shivers down my back at the same time. The Alcoholic finds me and somehow we end up in a room staring up at the ceiling to glow-in-the-dark stars. He tells me he loves me and then tries to make out, but the last thing I want is a tongue in my mouth. He gets mad, hightails it out, and I watch the fake big dipper glow bright on the ceiling.

Dusk is here and everyone wants to play Frisbee. I know it's gearing up to be time for the Atomic Hogs and I go outside to find the Alcoholic. Everyone is running, tossing the disc around, but I am coming down or getting tired or something that feels depressing. I sit on the side and watch as they play. Stash pulls a bottle of kerosene out of his back pocket, places it on his groin and sprays firewood with lighter fluid like he's pissing. Fake English Accent stumbles outside, hair a mess, tank top falling off her shoulder. She sits down next to me.

"Where's your boyfriend?" she asks.

"I don't know."

"Interesting."

We are quiet. The fire is small, but the flames are growing, and I can feel the edges of the heat trace my skin. I try to think of things to say to her, but nothing comes. She is barefoot. Her toenails are ragged, ripped up at the half moons. The sky is closing, melting into its final day colors: red, orange, blue. The sun is sinking below the belt, the waistline of the end of the world, dropping its weight on its toes. I want to find something funny or witty to say but my words are being swallowed with the daylight. I despise her and yet I want to impress her. She picks her cuticles and I look at the bandage around her hand.

"What happened?" I ask.

She points across the lawn to Booth House.

"See that window?"

She points up to Stash's broken pane.

"Yeah," I say.

"I put my hand through it, broke off a shard of glass and cut into my wrists."

"You tried to kill yourself?" I ask, staggered that she's shelling first-hand secrets to a stranger.

"What are you fucking crazy? You never cut yourself? You never took scissors to your legs, razors to your arms? Fuck, I just carved this a week ago."

She lifts her skirt to reveal her boyfriend's name BRENDAN scalpeled across her thigh.

"No," I say. "I never did that."

"Well, you should," she says. "It feels great."

It's dark. I want to find the Alcoholic, go see the band, and get the hell out of here. I remove myself politely from Fake English Accent and head down to the end of the world. There is only black and I can't see where it ends. I am anxious, panicky as I think about the burial ground, the disappearances, the insanity, but the winds have hours to go before they meet. I have never felt light before as I feel the darkness now. I am encased in a block of black ice, walking on the sky like the little boy in the night kitchen from that book when I was young. I remember that I have been here during the day, that it wasn't the end of my world. But the air is too thick, and I can't see what's in front of me. I bump into Stash as I race back to the dorm.

"What's the rush?" he says. "You're only running from yourself."

I laugh.

"Looking for your boyfriend?" he asks.

"Yeah. You seen him?"

"He's at the end of the world."

"Oh," I say.

"With some girl. You want me to walk with you?"

We walk down toward the end of the world in silence. I wonder which girl the Alcoholic is with, and my stomach turns as I imagine them, groping each other furiously before they are caught. Maybe they will turn into sand, be blown away. The grass is gathering frost; I hear the slight crunch under my feet. We are walking on cereal. I listen to the trees sway, the branches clacking together, prisoners banging on their lockup. The moon is behind us, behind a cloud, and it glows as a faint gold circle. My arms are crossed; my eyes are dry and achy. Is he with Sarah? With Fake English Accent? Did she somehow beat us to the end of the world?

I turn my head to see behind us. The dorms are lit up, the bonfire is blazing, but it is too dark to see the people playing Frisbee. I can't see if Fake English Accent is still sitting on the steps. The farther we get, the harder it becomes to see in front of us, behind. There is no light anywhere, just reminders of light, echoes. Everything looks like the insides of my eyelids—little white spotlights like constellations— and I blink to make certain my eyes are open. I know it makes no difference whether they are or aren't. I can't see ahead or behind me. It is as if the world has no sight. I am even uncertain if I am still walking, if Stash is still with me. I am so far into the darkness I have trouble balancing.

"Are you still here?" I say to Stash.

There is no response. My voice hangs there like I'm talking to myself.

"Stash?" I reach my hand out to the side to feel for a body.

Nothing.

Then suddenly,

"Do you know what I'm gonna do when we get to the end of the world?" he asks.

I am quiet for a second, wondering why he hadn't answered right away, but decide to let it go.

"No. What?" I ask.

He puts his hand on the back of my neck and clenches it hard.

"I'm going to rape you and then kill you," he says.

I stop walking and feel his grip tighten at the narrow of my neck. I become exhausted, so tired I think I might fall asleep. I have to force myself to react. I duck down fast and he loses his grip. I turn and start running back towards the dim glimmer of the dorms. I feel like I am running in place and I have to make myself keep going. My legs feel heavy and prickly like they are asleep, caught in a dream I am not having. It doesn't feel like running, what my body is doing, but the dorms are slowly coming into view so whatever I am doing must be right. I am breathing hard, or maybe not breathing at all, but I can hear Stash running behind me.

They are still playing Frisbee, I can hear them, and as I run someone starts to come into view. The dwarf is holding Sebby's baseball bat with the nails sticking out of it. He runs toward me, swinging the bat wildly as if to strike me. I am not sure what is real anymore, and I run choppy zigzag lines out of his range. He stops suddenly, turns and runs away. There is no sound. I think I am crying. Someone puts their hand on my shoulder. I am hoping to find the Alcoholic, but when I turn around, it's Stash. My eyes the height of his chest. I open my mouth to speak, but nothing escapes except a small white cloud of breath. His breath has staled to diesel fuel and when he bends down to me, I see his eyes have dilated out their color. He steadies my shoulders, like a guru adjusting a yoga pose, bends down and looks into my eyes. He doesn't say anything for a long time, just stares at me.

"You thought I was serious?" he finally says, still panting. "How could you think I was serious? I'm not a fucking psycho. I was just playing with you. I'm sorry," he says. "That was so wrong. I was kidding. I swear on my mother. It was a terrible joke. I know. I need therapy. I'm so so sorry. Please forgive me," he pleads.

I am still catching my breath, and can't speak. My teeth are clapping, applauding with an audience for a play I can't see. The cold comes in patches. The temperature is falling fast like a dead bird off a tree. I want to find the Alcoholic and drive home.

I thought my eyes would acclimate faster to the darkness the second time around, but it is just as hard to see. I am nervous we will go too far, fall off the end of the world. There are furious rushes of wind, followed by pockets of absolute stillness. The farther we go the deeper the silence. If you focus you can hear the layers of the atmosphere shifting. Sky becoming clouds becoming stars becoming planets. The quiet is profound; the smell is crisp, woody, burning charcoal and bark on fire. Dry leaves lift off the ground, encircle and smash each other in the wind. Branches bob, leaves flail like plastic bags caught in a wire fence. The gust pushes me from behind, pulls me into the mix. I am just another ingredient.

Stash is quiet. I don't want to engage him, and I don't want to think about the Alcoholic cheating on me with some tripping girl.

"You know what?" Stash asks suddenly.

"What?" I want to know.

"I killed your boyfriend," he says.

My heart lapses, maybe stops. Although I don't believe him my heart pounds anyway. He puts his hand on the back of my neck. Pushes a finger into the inlet, the pressure point at the base of my skull. I wonder, is this the nape? My voice is caught on branches.

"Stash. Stop it. You swore on your mother."

"My mother is dead. Quite a little fighter your boyfriend. What is he, a hundred thirty pounds? That little twerp didn't have a chance, and neither do you. I killed him and when we get to the end of the world, I'm going to kill you too." I struggle to get out from under his grip, but can't this time and he throws me onto the ground, sits on top of me. I start to scream for the Alcoholic but it comes out thin like a strained whisper, the last vestiges of coffee grinds being pushed through the filter.

I start crying, pleading with him. The things I say aren't even English. They are garbled words that need to be played backwards to be understood. I feel like a child as I scratch at him with my finger-nails. My nails are too short, useless. The pads of my fingers slide down his face. I smack at him. I feel the soft, flexible ridge of his ear. He holds my arms down on both sides, starts licking my face like a dog. The air blows cold on my wet cheeks, drying his licks up into a thin layer of second skin. I fling my face from side to side but he sits on my chest and presses his knee into the hollow of my neck. I feel like I'm choking, like there is a finger stuck down my throat. I make small gagging noises. His hands are big, wide and they hold my arms so tightly they feel stapled in place. The back of my head hurts where he threw me and I feel the throbbing tiny heartbeat in my skull. I am making noises I have never heard before. Animal noises. Retching, suf-focating noises. He presses his knee into my groin. Covers my mouth with his, jamming his entire tongue down my throat. He is clamped on me, his arm across my neck like a wrestler and I can barely breathe, much less move my head.

I try to vise my lips together, but his tongue has overtaken my mouth. I fold my tongue back, like I'm trying to swallow it, like I'm having an epileptic seizure, but he hooks his tongue around mine and pulls it back into place. He starts sucking on it so hard I think he might end up ripping it out of my mouth. I feel the string that connects my tongue at the base being pulled, and I imagine it fraying like a rope until it snaps off. He momentarily stops and I bite his lip hard. He curses at me and spits in my face. He is still holding my arms down and the spit has landed next to my nose. I want to wipe it off. I feel a small rock under me jutting into my rib and with every move he makes the deeper the rock goes. Digging all the way to my vertebrae. It pokes through my shirt, to my skin, through my skin, to the blood, through the blood to the bone, through the bone to the marrow. I wonder if I have brought this on myself.

Stash's face is charcoal gray. I am watching the skin melt off his face. He is just a skeleton, a bunch of overgrown bones. I see small fading light trails of his body pumping up and down beside him, behind him. With every movement he creates a new imprint of himself. There are at least ten of him now. All skulls, all bones.

Keeping me down with one foot on my chest, he unbuttons my pants and flips me onto my stomach. He tries pulling my pants down, but my hips are in the way, and they won't come off unless I lift my knees up. I don't. He grabs me by the hair and smacks my face into the dirt. My tooth has cut into my lip and it throbs in place. I taste the dirt in my mouth. It's knotty and crunchy like sand. My face is wet. He yanks my pants down with no regard for my hips and they chafe the outside of my thighs as he rips them down. He lifts my underwear off of me. I clench my cheeks together knowing this is going to make it worse for me, but I can't help it. I am writhing, but he is sitting on the backs of my knees and I can't move. I am a plank. I hear him unzip his pants. He lays himself on my back and I can feel his erection. He is thick, wide. I pray that he will prematurely ejaculate, but he doesn't. He pries my legs apart. He tries to stick himself in me, but he can't. I am rotating side to side like a snake, wriggling from underneath him. Every time he tries to enter me he misses, curses, smacks me in the back of the head. I almost want to help him, get him in me, make him come and get this over with, but I don't. I don't lie still.

He is prying me apart now, both hands on my rear, tearing into the skin with his fingernails trying to find his way in. My arms, I suddenly realize, are free. I bend them at the elbow and throw my fists back as hard as possible. I feel his face on my knuckles. He grabs himself lifting up, and I roll over fast and get him off me. I kick his face. He curses at me. I am crawling. Kneeling. Standing.

As I run I pull my pants up. It feels unnaturally slow, but I race. My body feels heavy. My legs ache, my head aches, my skin aches. But I run faster than I have ever run in my life. I burn up the grass, running and taking the whole world with me, the end of the world, the beginning. I am dragging it with me: to show to friends, to bury with relatives. I can run the five hours back to school; I can run with the Alcoholic on my back. I am alive. I am dead.

I near the dorm. Soil, grass, and tears stuck to my jeans, my elbows, my hair. There are two figures on the front steps. A couple of guys are tossing the disc back and forth over the fading bonfire. The rest are gone, off to see the band. The people on the front steps are passing a bottle of liquor between them. The wind is thickening, stiffening behind me. It is trying to suck me back in, into the end of the world, but I run with the weight of my body forward, withdrawing myself from it.

I approach the dorm and the people on the front step focus. The Alcoholic is not dead. He is not even hurt. The Alcoholic is sitting with Fake English Accent. No scratches. He is laughing and she is laughing. They don't see me. He looks at his watch and taps his leg. I know he is waiting for me, but he is not looking for me.

I can hear the Atomic Hogs playing in the distance and they don't even sound good to me anymore. They sound like what they are, a pointless college band. I don't feel like a student anymore. I don't feel like much of anything. All I know is that everyone looks a little bit different. Even the Alcoholic. He looks needy and unhealthy. In this moment and for the next moments thereafter I see everyone clearly, everyone here is flat, trying, posing, reaching. It is the day after someone dies, when you see everything as if for the first time because the world has new meaning without them. The grass, the trees, the weather. I see the moment in things: the exertion of grass, the rootlessness of birds. And then the instant escapes me and everything returns as it was before. There is no meaning behind trees, nothing poignant about the sky. Everything remains. Except me, I think. I am the one who is different.

I stand in front of the Alcoholic. I don't say a word, I just stand there, and he and Fake English Accent look up. I don't care about Fake English Accent anymore, about making an impression, about her liking me. I don't care about anything anymore. I just want to go home, even though I am not quite sure what that means now. The Alcoholic opens his mouth to say something to me, but I walk away, head toward the parking lot. I open the passenger side door and sit, knees up, on the floor of the front seat.

How I feel now is like floating. I see the Alcoholic as if I am looking down, I watch him open the car door with a detached horror. But I'm not flying. I'm hiding, holding my knees to my chest, expecting someone else might scoop me up, take me away. It all started as an explosion, and we on earth are just riding the debris.

GETTING RID OF THEM

We haven't talked about kids. Not raising them or getting rid of them. The Alcoholic has been abused, beaten by his parents, pushed down stairs, chased after with a butcher knife. He is fragile, scared. He wants kids, that much I know. I'm just not sure what he'll do to them once he has them. The Alcoholic knows about getting smacked. I've never asked him if he'd hit the kids. I just make sure we're careful. His parents have a dog and I've seen the Alcoholic whack him from time to time. He does it in private, when he thinks no one is looking, and I suppose he thinks that makes all the difference. I yell at him. We fight about the dog, but it isn't about the dog at all.

He has stories. When he was a teenager his mother cracked a bottle open, chased him around with the serrated edge, held it up to his cheek and pressed it into his soft pubescent stubble.

"That's where the scar's from," he says.

His mom was volatile as a firearm. She'd turn on a dime, knock him senseless then apologize once the bleeding stopped. I take care of him now.

We are twenty-five and my other friends are ready. They want kids: one, three, maybe even four. They crave children like the tin man his heart. Me, I'm not entirely sure. It doesn't hunger me, keep me up nights. I'm indifferent. Not to children, to thoughts of having them. I keep quiet on the matter. Sometimes I feel like I've already lived my life, raised my kids and am waiting to embrace the softness that comes with old age. There are no surprises left. I pass people on the street sensing I've seen them all before. I know the sag in each awning, the smell of someone else's nostalgia, the name of every fracture in the sidewalk. I recognize the weather before it falls.

The future, the past, they merged somewhere for me. Each day has been lived before, a premonition of every tomorrow. All the days are Monday through Sunday, every night lived out in bars.

On Tuesday night the Alcoholic and I go out with the Best Friend. The three of us play pool, drink Guinness, talk about the downtown music scene. We're at our favorite watering-hole, the Holiday Fever. The Best Friend is on hiatus from his girlfriend and he's trying out the flirting thing. His conversations are banter, eyes arched in a perpetual roll, mouth twisted into an incessant grin. He thinks that "chicks dig it," but they don't.

The Alcoholic takes a lucky shot, banks the four ball in the corner pocket. He looks up at me for approval. I raise my eyebrows like a question.

"Didn't you see that?" he asks.

"Yeah," I say.

"It was good, right?"

"Yeah, honey. It was good."

He smiles, and then misses the next ball. The Best Friend gets the black one in, racks up another game. The bar door swings open and a couple in their mid twenties fall through the threshold. They are rock-star-like. She's stuffed into black leather pants and a tank top with three rips across the chest, like a superhero busting out of his day clothes. The guy has a hoop in his nose, a gold front tooth, and wears a stocking headband that holds back the outgrowth of his platinum-dyed hair. They near me, trying to maintain a straight line, but trip over each other as they edge toward the back table. Her shirt has letters in rainbow script across the breasts: *Easy on the Eyes*. Her stomach distends below it, creating a space between the bottom of her shirt and the top of her pants. Her belly button pops out like the thermometer on a microwave chicken and it takes me a long minute before I realize she's pregnant.

She slides into the booth behind ours. He writes his name in chalk on the board by the pool table.

"Wolfie," she whines. "Get me a drink."

Wolfie shuffles over to the bar, turns around, says,

"Whaddya want, babe?"

"The usual, babe. Don't you remember anything?"

"Sorry, babe," he says. And then to the bartender,

"A Tequila Sunrise for the missus."

The Alcoholic is losing this round and it looks like the Best Friend is gonna have to play Wolfie. The Alcoholic polishes the end of his pool stick, looks at me, winks. I smile, winking back. He takes a shot at the four and misses. He doesn't meet my eye for the rest of the game. Wolfie drops the Tequila Sunrise in front of the missus and hovers over to the Best Friend who is lining up the eight ball. He concentrates. As he pulls back his pool stick to strike it, Wolfie yells,

"Don't miss!" The ball goes flying in the wrong direction and knocks the cue ball in by accident. His game is lost and he's pissed. The Best Friend wants to start something and heads over to Wolfie, but Wolfie is hobbled, bent left instead of giving his whole weight to both feet. The Best Friend catches Wolfie's eyes as he nears and when he sees all life sucked out from them, he begs off.

We see the couple the day after that and the day after that. They keep checking in to the Holiday Fever like it's the Holiday Inn. The third time they come in the missus wears a pink ribbed tank top with the name *Lisa* across the chest in gold decals. She is very disco. I'm not sure if they recognize us because we're never met with acknowledgment. I wonder if they see us at all. Lisa packs herself into the back booth and Wolfie goes up to the bar.

"Wolfie," she snivels. "Get me a drink."

Wolfie tottles his way to the bar, turns around, says,

"Whaddya want, babe?"

"The usual, babe. Don't you remember anything?"

"Sorry, babe," he says. And then to the bartender,

"A Tequila Sunrise for the Missus."

Me, I'll never forget her drink.

This third time she's fidgety. She looks every which way like she's watching for surveillance cameras. She scratches herself with enough might she leaves raised red trails on her arms and she's squirming about in the vinyl booth like there are bugs on her skin. Wolfie drops the Tequila Sunrise in front of her and goes to watch the Best Friend kick the Alcoholic's ass in pool. *Lisa* takes a sip or two of her Tequila Sunrise, then heads to the bathroom. It's been five, ten, fifteen minutes since she went to the bathroom. Wolfie doesn't seem to notice her disappearance. The Alcoholic's waiting his turn for a shot so I go up behind him and kind of whisper into his neck.

"That girl's been gone a long time."

"What girl?" he asks.

"The girl who's with Wolfie," I say annoyed.

"Who's Wolfie?"

"Just forget it."

I walk down the short hall. The ladies' bathroom door is shut. I knock but there's no answer. I wait a minute, knock again. Still nothing.

"Hello?" I say.

"*Lisa?*" I call.

"Anyone?"

I try the handle. It turns. I open it slowly, giving her a chance to say something, to call out that she's on the can and hang on a sec, but there's no noise. The door is buoyant, almost weightless, and without even a push it glides open exposing the dank, sticky room, the smell of stale piss. She's on the can all right. She's on the can but her pants aren't down. Her body leans all the way over, like she's in italics. Her head rests against the wall. One arm is on the toilet paper dispenser; the other is on her stomach. Her eyes are closed like she's asleep except her lips are blue. I look down at her stomach. There's a needle sticking out of it. A needle where the baby is.

I watch from the stoop as they load her onto a gurney, into the back of the ambulance. The syringe still sticks out of her pregnant belly as they roll her out of the bar. Wolfie's in a daze so the bouncer pushes him toward the ambulance. He's holding a pool stick as he closes himself into the van. The Alcoholic and the Best Friend stand outside watching, shaking their heads back and forth like they knew this was coming, like they know all about her kind.

We see them a couple weeks later. She is still pregnant, which for some reason strikes me as odd. She comes in first, before Wolfie. She's got on a halter-top that just barely covers her breasts. Silver studs trace the top lip of the fabric. Her stomach is hard and round like a basketball. A Band-Aid lies above her belly button resembling an eyebrow, and I think, that's it?

I want to talk to her, see how she's doing, but she has that look. Her face doesn't see anything past the drink. I want to know if it was a mistake. If she just missed her arm and got her stomach. I want to know who she was trying to get rid of, the baby or herself. I walk by her table, smile at her. She looks through me like I'm cellophane.

The Alcoholic and the Best Friend are at the Jukebox. The Alcoholic air guitars and the Best Friend sings. *Some people call me the Space Cowboy, yeah, some call me the gangster of love . . .* I rack up a new game of pool, stare at *Lisa* and wonder who she'll give her baby to once it's born.

Wolfie comes in and tosses a backpack into the booth with *Lisa*. She doesn't look at him either. She's staring at the wall, looking at the space where the warning sign about drinking while pregnant hangs. She's fixed on that spot and I wonder does she even see the sign? Wolfie looks at me, puts a couple quarters down on the table.

"You wanna play?" he asks.

"Sure," I say, "you break."

Wolfie's an ace at breaking. The balls go dancing off all corners, and he gets in two high balls. I'm solid, which sort of bums me out because lately I've been lucky with the stripes. Wolfie sucks down cigarettes as easily as beer and he's running off to the bathroom every five minutes so I'm thinking he must be doing coke too. I have every opportunity to cheat, to push in a couple of low balls with my hand, make a few more of my balls disappear every time he does, but I don't. I'm a little bit scared of Wolfie. The Alcoholic and the Best Friend are sitting at the end of the bar. They're writing lyrics down on a cocktail napkin, thinking they're the next Jim Morrison. They sound out their songs, try out a couple harmonies. They're like those girls I hate who clasp hands and sing as they skip down the street. I feel embarrassed for them and wait for Wolfie to return.

Wolfie's been gone a while now and I think to myself, oh no, not again. I see *Lisa* make a move to get up and I hope she's going to check on her man, but she wanders over to me, looks right at my belly. Her eyes have black rings around them like she hasn't washed off her make-up since she started wearing it when she was ten. She puts her cold hand on my stomach and says,

"How many months are you?"

I look at her confused, like maybe she's delusional, putting off her pregnancy on me.

"I'm not pregnant," I respond.

"That's what you think," she says and walks off to the bathroom to get Wolfie.

We don't see them for a week or so and I start getting worried. But one night we walk in there and it's packed with college students from around the globe as if word got out about the best kept secret in New York. I figure Wolfie and Lisa are trolling some other bar waiting for the hype to die. We start going to International until things cool down at Holiday Fever. International doesn't have a pool table so it gets dull fast and we sit side by side at the bar looking at ourselves in the mirror for a time.

I get the first of the cramps a week later at Sweet and Vicious. We're sitting in this nice garden with bamboo trees and wooden benches, when I feel this pulling, this slight tugging like a cat pressing his paws against the inside of my stomach. I try and remember when I last got my period, but I'm not organized about these things. I don't keep track of my bank account, my bills, my cycle. I attempt the math, but for the life of me, I can't remember. Maybe I'm due for my period, I think. Maybe I'm ovulating. I figure I'll find out soon enough. I order a vodka tonic which eases the pain, gets my mind on something else.

We find this other bar, one with a TV, whose remote, for some reason, is in our charge. We are watching some sitcom, some bad excuse for a comedy, when I get the pains again. The cramps are dull at first, easy to ignore, but then they mount, the seizing becomes abrupt. The space between assaults tapers like the interval between thunder lashes, but nothing comes out of me. The Alcoholic sees something's wrong and he gets me a shot of whiskey to dull the spasms. He thinks it's my period. I'm starting to think it's not.

We come back the next night and the next because to be honest we start getting hooked on "E!" I like seeing what people wear to the awards shows and the Alcoholic likes seeing the Behind the Scenes stuff. The Best Friend pretends he doesn't care about any of it, but I see him perk up when they show people walking down the red carpet. Some famous actors are getting married and after the commercial break they're gonna talk about who's coming, what they're gonna wear. I don't want to miss that segment.

Suddenly, there's a clamp on me, in place of the cramps and it feels like it's bracing, tightening its hold. It's five minutes later when I get the next jolt, then three, then two, then one. It's a countdown, but to what, I'm not sure.

I make my way to the bathroom hunched over like a flaccid carrot. I sit on the toilet wondering what this is, also kind of hoping I'm not missing the segment on the celebrities. There is a metal bar attached to the wall and I grab it every time I have a cramp. I try not to make a noise, but it's almost unbearable, like someone is putting a live wire to a nerve ending, and a soprano shaped moan escapes from my throat. A couple of tears fall off the globes of my cheeks and I watch them hit the ground like people jumping off their sinking ship.

I wonder if I've been poisoned, have a parasite. Maybe I have something tropical, maybe even AIDS. My tee shirt clings with sweat to my chest. There's heaviness, a slow dropping like falling colors in a lava lamp. The water in the toilet splashes. I'm dizzy, weightless, queasy. I am afraid to look, scared of what I'll see. But it's just blood, clumps of blood, and it keeps pouring out of me like a bowl of red soggy cereal. I sit there for a while really suffering. I figure the longer I'm gone, the more certain it'll be that the Alcoholic will come help me. But the thing is, he doesn't.

I finally finish bleeding out, but just to be on the safe side, I stuff a wad of toilet paper in my underwear. The Alcoholic and the Best Friend are still sitting at the bar and the Alcoholic looks at me and says,

"What the hell were you doing in there, giving birth?"

A few weeks later I make an appointment with a doctor who sends me to an OB-GYN who does an ultrasound or a sonogram. She condescends about not knowing my period schedule, for considering the pull out method protected sex. Then she hands me a bunch of pamphlets on safe sex and abortion. She says it was an early miscarriage, not late, or threatened or incomplete or whatever else kind of miscarriages there are. For some reason, I don't believe her, mainly because I didn't know I was pregnant. I watch her like she's a commercial, waiting for the talking to stop so I can get on with the show. It sinks in, and after a couple of days, I do kind of believe her. I cry myself to sleep for a few nights, hoping the Alcoholic will hear me, wake up and ask what's wrong. He never does and because of that I decide to keep it to myself for awhile.

I am sad for the baby and sad for me. I think about what the kid would have looked like, if it was a boy or a girl. I imagine a girl, and I see us now in the hospital, my mother and father, the Alcoholic and his parents, all of them standing over the baby and me, looking at us like we were the only miracles in the world. She has light tufts of strawberry blonde hair, and tiny pink fingers that want only to be opened. I make a room for her in this tiny apartment, a space for her in this bed. And then, accidentally, I identify her. Unconsciously and against all real wishes, I name her. With her name she takes my whole heart and I see clearly now it's been hollowed. But then I see the white plastic chairs and the curtain being drawn around me and the doctor with his mask staring down at me with contempt. He wouldn't be gentle as he scraped the lining, grated the baby right out of me. I wonder what would have happened had I been given the choice.

Things are stronger now; my feelings are all gold. I can smell a pacifier from a block away.

We're back at Holiday Fever because a new bar is getting all the hype. There are regulars at the counter, sharks ready to pounce the pool table. They nod and smile when I walk past them. It's a special type of loneliness being this familiar in a bar.

I see Wolfie come in, then a minute later, *Lisa*. She is wearing a regular white, boy's Hanes tee shirt and a pair of cutoff shorts. But the most distinctive thing about her is the newborn baby. She shows it to everyone as she walks in, even strangers.

"Look at our baby," she says to the customers and holds him out for show.

"Isn't he cute?" she asks the bartender.

"What's his name?" someone calls out.

"He doesn't have one yet," she says. "Any ideas?"

Then people start yelling out names left and right, good names, bad names, funny names. They are screaming like on the floor of the stock exchange: Peter! Tony! Tumor! Loser! Freakboy! Truck! Romeo! People are really getting into it, even the Alcoholic and the Best Friend. They are thinking up names as if it's their own kid. But I have no names for him.

Lisa and Wolfie sit in the back booth with their baby. They take visitors who fondle and coo at their little boy. They claw him with their cigarette stained fingers, breathe on him with their hot Guinness breath. I get up and head toward the bathroom, but when I reach their table, *Lisa* looks up, holds her baby toward me. I reach out and touch his head.

"He's beautiful," I say.

His little hand is curled shut and I gently unfold his fingers. I stroke his little palm and he clasps his entire hand around my index finger, claiming it as his own. His eyes are tiny incisions sealed shut. Lisa exhales a thin veil of smoke, and I wonder how she could have possibly known. How could someone like her have seen through me? They pass a joint back and forth across the baby's face and Wolfie dips a finger in his beer, sticks the foam in the baby's mouth. When the little lip curves up, Wolfie laughs, spit pasting his gold tooth. Wolfie's mouth is all there is now, a wide gaping mine shining like a fortune. It burns, glowing until there is nothing left of him but precious yellow metal. I gently remove my finger from the baby's hand and walk away to the bathroom wondering if I'll ever be so lucky.

CLOSING MY EYES AND LETTING HIM DO IT

Your hair is a mess; everyone talks about how greasy it is. Another reflection on me, I suppose. It took me three months to realize you were using conditioner, not shampoo.

At home it's just the three of us: you, me, and the cravings. They're like French fries you say, can't have just one. The penny jar is empty, no more quarters in the couch, under the bed. The vacuum bag is drained, going through all my pockets, pants I've never worn. Laundry basket's upside down; bed sheets turned inside out. Dimes in the floorboard gouged out by a knife.

You won't remember tomorrow like you don't remember all the girls you've fucked, like you don't remember to come home some nights. The sun arrives on the fire escape, warms up the soft empty streets. He's dead, he's dead, he's dead, I think, repeating the words like a mantra, an artificial heartbeat. In the morning when you return mute, flailing, quick to shower before explaining, you'd think I'd had enough. I am just starting, and you are not dead, but perhaps you should be. At least then I would have gotten your Molly Hatchett tee shirt.

You said you'd lay down and die for me. You shadow me to every inch of my life. Can't go to the bathroom without you standing outside its door. You tell me you love me at every commercial, fourteen times in a row, each time meaning less than before.

At night you spoon me to suffocation, gets so I dread going down, getting my rest. You grab on tight when I try to roll over. When you want it you climb on me as I'm drifting to sleep, turn my dreams into deception. I could be the sock you jerk off into. You cry when I don't want to, say you're too ugly for me to love. Sometimes you say you'll end it all, cut your body to bits with a knife until I concede. You pin my arms over my head and I give up, give in, closing my eyes, and letting you do it.

A REGULAR VIRGIN MARY

The Alcoholic said I was the still point in his spinning world. The adhesive in a city held together by Band-Aids. Everything here slips off; the hard-hats are all waiting to fall. They like the job for the view. They'll be toppled one day, crushed by a city they can't save. All the streets are under construction, there are scaffolds and cranes and the weight of the summer's heat is tearing out my breath.

We have two knapsacks and are piling bricks into them for bookshelves. It was the Alcoholic's idea, but it took him two days to drag me from bed. The world is getting smaller; the wrong people are in control. He's taken to stealing things he believes should be free, like shelves. People watched as we climbed over the fence, broke into the construction site. It's Sunday, so the workmen aren't here to yell at us, run us out with mallets.

I said things never change, but the Alcoholic pointed to the orange cones, the anchor bolts, the danger men working sign, buildings being torn down to be built back up, and said,

"Right there babe, is proof that you're wrong."

I have been having panic attacks. The last one was two weeks long so I cut my arms up to keep my body from floating away. The space we live in is three hundred fifty square feet with a shower in the kitchen and a roommate on the couch. We're shielded only by sight behind a thin hanging towel. He wakes me at three, four, five in the morning, ropes me in for sex and cigarettes. We used to smoke all our cigarettes together—before bed, in bed. We'd wake up for cigarettes two, three times a night. In the morning, it'd be the first thing we reached for. Now it's just him that keeps the routine. I am smoked out. I still reach for the stick, but I am slowing down.

The cans of spilled beer attract baby roaches and I buy flip-flops because the ground sticks to me when I walk. The shower tiles are filling with black green fungus; I buy a mat to avoid stepping in it. He forgets to clean up but I'm done. Now, I let the cockroaches crawl into his clothes, settle, lay eggs in his thug hat.

Some people are saying I'm depressed, but I'm just tired. There are days when I realize I have forgotten to eat, completely overlooked it as if it were something to be remembered, jotted down in a book. My stomach never growls, my internal clocks have been reset, turned off, melted down to oil from the summer's humidity. Grease and cheese dribble down chins at Ray's Pizza but they'll just get hungry again, returning over and over to this corner for slice after slice, never accepting hunger can't be satisfied. I could sleep all day if it weren't for the earth's rotation, the daily grind of light through these windows. I could stay coiled under sheets and pillows if the city didn't shriek and burn from morning till morning, day in day out. I could do it all from here, I think. Plan my plans and dream my dreams. Occasionally I go downstairs, sit on the bench in the playground, watch the girls double dutch. They have it all. *A is for Anna who lives in Alabama and she eats Apple Strudel and her best friend is Alice.* The day they wave goodbye to me I feel it. I am becoming a fixture. Like any hydrant, soon the dogs will piss on me.

By the last week of June, with no air conditioner, we are living a squatter's life and the Alcoholic couldn't be happier. For some reason I let him think I've been looking for a job, dressing and primping, conquering the concrete, handing my resume out like a flyer on the corner of Mulberry and Lin's Korean Deli. He feels for me, rails against the recession, the worst job market our country's seen since blah blah blah, the baby boomers, the stock market, and other things he says when he's the only one listening. Perhaps I should tell him I've been lying before he writes a third person account, tries to get his thoughts published. Maybe I'll say nothing, ride the diatribes out for one more week, one more month.

We brush our teeth in the kitchen sink. Toothpaste spit is clogging up the drain. I'm not sure why there are dirty dishes in the first place. We never cook, but there they are, crusty and growing food of their own. One day I think, throw them all out. So, I do.

Some nights the Alcoholic doesn't come home until two, three, four in the morning. He is getting dirtier. His hair seems oilier with each washing. Fast food is the only food he ingests and his skin is starting to show for it. He is bun colored, growing mold instead of facial hair. A happy hour devotee, a rock-n-roll heartache, a dirty boy, a drunk. Mornings turn dark on me when I start staying in bed till night. By the end of that last week in June it takes my eyes an hour to adjust to light. I have been in bed for seven days.

"What's your problem?" he says.

"Nothing. I'm just tired."

"You've been tired for months," he says.

I've been tired for years, I think.

"Well, what about me?" he says.

"What about you?"

"Never mind," he says and storms off.

I am starting to love him a total of an hour a week. He is most alive on stage, but the gigs are getting fewer and farther between. We talk about his sobriety, or lack thereof. His last bender was three days long. This time he says he's gonna make it. But why should today be different from any other? And I am right because two weeks later, he's back to bingeing.

He got the number off a flyer on a stop sign on Ridge and Rivington and within forty-five minutes a bike messenger is knocking at our door. Inside of a shoebox are twenty plastic containers, normally used to store paper clips. The stuff in the red box is hydro, he explains, it's the strongest. The Alcoholic gives him sixty bucks for the pot and the stolen office supply. He drags me out of bed and from the fire escape we watch the tops of people's heads go by. We toke slowly off the perfectly smooth joint he rolled.

It's strong, so I take only two or three hits. The Alcoholic takes more. The distance between the fire escape and the street begins to melt away and I feel the metal grate give underneath me until I am sinking into the sidewalk, submerged into the city block. I look up to buildings leaning over, the sky closing in. Behind the sky is another dimension, dogs and plastic ducks, a heaven for pets and toys. I see a big wheel, a sit n' spin, a Fisher Price Pixelvision camera, all floating in a dimension that isn't there.

I turn to the Alcoholic and he sees it too, the sky, the toys, and maybe something else altogether. Across the street windows are melting down sides of buildings, the facade surges and curls like the ocean. Foam drips, bricks buckle, and streets are all torn down. I am on a float in a parade, waving like the mayor. We are riding the fire escape to anywhere. And then I feel something I've never felt before: I could be important, famous even. I am being held back by invisible reins, or are they? There might be a pedestal out there waiting for me to amount to something. I see it all then, like a vision, a regular Virgin Mary. There is something other than pot in this pot.

I look at the Alcoholic but he is long gone. He will beat his kids. I can see it. I look at the Alcoholic and it shines, like a vision, a regular Second Coming. It's over. Even though he is with me, I am alone. We spend our lives ignoring the data only to have it all catch up with us some hot July day as we're staring high at our lover wondering where it all went wrong.

When the sun drips and the moon glides in, the Alcoholic makes a run for a twelve pack and a fifth of something. He needs a kick; he is scared of life when he's not high. He likes to drink before he drinks. Does a couple shots before going to a bar. Downs the first few drinks fast just so he can catch a quick buzz. He doesn't like the effects of anything to take its time. The liquor store guy knows him, gives him a discount every two weeks, so tonight he returns with a case of beer, a full bottle of whiskey. Has me lay on his lap while he pours a couple of shooters into my mouth. I am lying here looking up at him, swallowing liquor that sears my mouth, thinking *what the fuck am I doing?* I sit up before it's too late, before I'm too drunk to take it back. I sit up and the Alcoholic looks at me, grins, says,

"My turn."

He wants me to unload the whole thing down his throat, but I won't do it. So he grabs the bottle from me, lifts it over his head, tilts his face all the way back and watches the liquid waterfall into his mouth. He's half way through the bottle when he stops, gets his speech face. As he turns to me, he accidentally kicks a fresh pack of cigarettes through the bars of the fire escape. We watch it fall to the ground with a silent thlump. He says,

"This is it."

"What?" I say.

"This." He holds up the bottle like a trophy.

"Tonight's my last bender," he says. "Tomorrow, I'm done. Quitting the drink, but tonight, I'm going hog wild."

"Quite the Politician."

"I mean it. This is it. I'm done, finished. You don't know what it's like, being inside this body all the time, wanting out and wanting out, and the only way to do it is to drink my way there. I don't want to do it. Not anymore. I want to be responsible, to have people at work point at me saying, he's your man. If there's a proper guy for the hard-est job, then pick that kid, him right there. I know how you see me, how everyone sees me. You think I can't feel it, but I can. Your thoughts are like cartoon bubbles. I can read them all the time. So tonight, this is it. I celebrate my newfound sobriety, because as of tomorrow, I am cutting myself off."

"Are you real?" I ask, suspicious.

"Yes, ma'am. As real as the color of horse shit."

I have heard it before and each time I chose to believe it, but not like tonight. I have never heard him speak so clearly, and because of that, the arrangement of his sentences, the rhythm of his delivery, I don't make a choice to believe it, I actually do. Maybe now, if he asks me to marry him, I'll say yes and mean it and want it.

He spends the rest of the night getting tanked, and I spend the rest of the night letting him.

He drinks the remaining whiskey, drinks the entire case of beer. One after another after another. By three in the morning he is so drunk I'm thinking he might be poisoned. But he's not done. He smokes more of the pot, looks at me, cocks an eyebrow, gets serious, gives a speech. All the while, his arms are flailing, over-gesticulating as if his limbs were making the points instead of his words.

"You know it, right? That you're the only thing in the world that keeps me alive, right? That you are more me than I am. That I can't live if you're not here. I know more about you than you do about yourself. I'm like God that way, get it? Like God. You're like . . . you're like . . . my little angel and I need to protect you. We need each other. We're like one person, get it? Without you I have no start or finish, no beginning or end, because you are it. My line to cross, my ready set go. You know what I'm talking about here? You are my entire life. You know if you leave me, I'll fucking kill myself, right? How's that to have hanging over your head. Now you can't ever leave, because you know it's true. I'll fucking drown my fucking self, shoot my brains out on the Williamsburg Bridge. Fuck, I'll tape the whole thing just so you can watch it every day and know what you did to me. You are my whole world. Can't you see that? You know what I'm saying here, right? You can't leave me. You're in this forever, right? This is it for me. It's it for you too, right? Right?"

Now he's crying, got his arms wrapped around my waist and he's sobbing, making me make promises I don't want to keep. But I pledge it because he won't remember this tomorrow. In five minutes he's on the fire escape, puking over the side of the railing three floors high, on top of the cigarettes he dropped, the years of invisible footprints, dead souls smudged and buried into dirt on this very same block of Manhattan, 10012.

I wake up the next day not knowing how I got into bed. My head feels like a wood block, carved out, etched into a still life with a paring knife. I look at the calendar to see what day we're up to and it's July 4th. Independence Day. The birth of our country, the birth of my life. Today is my birthday. I am twenty-seven years old.

He's got a gig tonight, and before we leave he gives me my present: a whip and a dog collar. For a minute I wait, ready for the puppy that belongs to the dog collar, but when he says, "try it on," I realize it's for me to wear. This couldn't be less me, and I wonder which porn star is walking around naked. I stare at it, wondering how he could be so wrong, how he could know me this little after so long. I ask him where he got it. He says,

"Uh . . . I don't remember, I'll ask Angela."

"Why would she know?

"Well, she helped pick it out."

"She did? So, should I call her to thank her?"

"Why are you mad?"

"I just think it's a little weird that you went to a sex store with another woman."

"Angie's a lesbian."

"Oh, I see," I say. "So that makes her not a girl?"

He is annoyed with me.

"You see. I can't do anything right."

I don't answer.

The gig is at nine. His bandmates are already setting up when we get there at eight thirty. All their girlfriends get things that suit them: thrift store finds, flea market rings, the occasional suede jacket. But me, I have a whip and a dog collar waiting on the edge of my bed. The presents he gives me resemble his love: inadvertent, thoughtless. I don't want to be here. I don't want to be anywhere but in bed watching the blue sky taper black.

I stand in the back while they tune their guitars. It is crowded. Overflowing with couples. The Alcoholic stands in the corner talking to his drummer. Then the bass player joins in. They point to some imaginary spot onstage, nod their heads, smile, look over at me. I wonder what the hell they're talking about, why they're looking at me, but I smile back, not really giving that much of a shit anymore about anything. The Alcoholic has a beer in his hand and as he drinks it, he catches my eye, shrugs. His promises last hours; mine last years. He doesn't care that he has a drinking problem, he doesn't care that he's ruining his life, our relationship. Up until now maybe I didn't either, but I'm more exhausted than I've ever been, and looking at him now, I finally see it. We've both given up.

The bass player jumps up on stage, then the drummer; they start tuning up, bearing down. The Alcoholic whispers something to the bartender, then something to the light guy. He jumps up on stage and I feel a rush, a sudden high of love for him. The spotlight shines down on the Alcoholic.

They play four songs in a row before addressing the audience. Everyone in the crowd knows all words, sings along, even me, and I love him, would do anything to keep him this way forever. His voice carries clear and round across the wood floor, climbs right up my legs, settling into my skin like a fairy tale. People are thumping their feet, clapping their hands, rocking out, all for the Alcoholic and the exquisite noise he makes. Liquor is spilled, mugs of ale are held high in cheers. The Alcoholic plays the one everyone loves, the one about me, "She's My One Hit Wonder." And when he's done, he nods to the bartender, motions to the sound guy, the light guy, and everything changes.

The lights go red and just on him, the bartender stands on the bar, the sound guy turns off all the mics except for the Alcoholic's. The Bartender, in a low stunning voice, starts singing "Amazing Grace" and the Alcoholic bends down on one knee. He holds the microphone in front of his mouth and says,

"Honey, will you marry me?"

Everyone turns around, looks at me. The Best Friend, his grin and a pint of ale raised, a girl in a black tube top whose insincere smile barely disguises deep creases of jealousy, the bartender, the light guy, the drunk in the corner. Everyone is stuck like mannequins in awkward poses not meant to be held and I wonder if they'll ever move again. Their gaping mouths could catch flies and I wonder if time has stood still all over the world, or just here in this bar. Shiny faces, gelled hair, sweat pellets, acne, yellow teeth. I see only the worst features in everyone. My skin feels numb with all these eyes on it. A girl in the front raises her eyebrows, motions for me to speak. Someone yells out,

"Where's the ring?"

Things reverse: the proverbial record scratch undoes itself, heads turn back to the stage, chairs swivel back into place, the tap flows and the Alcoholic gets flustered, says,

"Uh. I don't have one yet."

He pauses, looks at me from across the bar, from on that stage, takes a swig of beer, says,

"Is that a yes or a no?"

I can't say anything, I am on the spot, and all I can manage is to nod my head, yes. Everyone breaks into applause and the Alcoholic comes off stage, gives me a hug. It's the best gig he ever played and the one I hate the most.

Afterwards we stand together, posing in our newfound happiness. He accepts shots of whiskey, pints of beer. But me, I drink nothing, say nothing. People congratulate us, and I play along showing off the invisible engagement ring he didn't buy me that is not on my finger. He has his arm too tight around me. I couldn't get out from under him even with pliers.

He wants to go to the river, check out the fireworks, but I want to go home. I am on the verge of tears, of bawling, and I don't know why. I have been holding it in for too long, and my chest feels dented from the strain. I tell him to go, to meet me at home, but surprisingly, he says he'll pass, come home with me. We're engaged after all, is what he says. We should do everything together. All I can think is no, no, no, no, no. But I say nothing. I don't do anything at all.

At home, I get back in bed, stare at the wall. When he walks into the room it takes me over, I can't hold it in anymore and I just start crying. I unleash years worth of tears, untether right there like a baby girl falling apart in her crib. He doesn't know what to do, how to care for me, he just keeps saying,

"What's the matter? What'd I do?"

But I can't do it anymore. Because now it's gone further than it ever should have. One more false word from me and I'll wear that dog collar as he drags me from year to year by a leash. Is life worth living when you've let someone else choose the life you're to lead? I can't tell him nothing's the matter, that I love him, will always love him, will never leave him. I can't keep pacifying him when I need consoling. I am spent. At the end of all ropes. I am separate from my body now, hovering over both of us from the ceiling. My voice, just a detached vehicle from which words are formed. For the first time ever, I say it. I call him a drunk. And for the first time ever, he doesn't disagree. It all comes out, little by little, then more, then all. I am choking and talking at the same time. I wonder if I am saying words at all. Behind my blubbering, all my sounds come out like bolts, dropping dead and lifeless to the floor. I tell him how tired I am, how drained. That I can't keep faking it. There is nothing left of me.

Once I was a strongbox, packed, filled to capacity with valuables, but now I am empty, unusable, broken. I tell him I can't take anymore. His drinking has depleted me, emptied me of myself. That after all is said and drank, I don't know who I am. I look in the mirror and I see someone with no name. I am outside myself, looking over my shoulder whispering, that's you? Are you sure? There is no connection when I look at myself, none whatsoever. I feel like a self-portrait of someone else, someone I recognize, but can't place. Like a B movie star, died young. I have never been so far gone before.

And he listens. He listens as I tell him I can't marry a drunk. That as much as I am terrified of being alone I am better off solo than spending my life with someone who barely exists. I think about the streets, the city blocks, the parking lots being torn down to be built back up into co-ops and condos and I think, that's me. I am just some dumb plot of land the Alcoholic claimed. But now, I need to be leveled and razed, rebuilt by my own hands. He says,

"But what about me? Are you still gonna marry me?"

I say,

"Only if you're sober."

I never called anyone a drunk before. I never sent anyone to AA, but I have never been so tired in all my life. That night I cried from the exhaustion of being with him. He said he'd get sober, get himself clean if it meant being with me. He said he'd go to the meetings, get a sponsor, twelve step the drink right out of him. He said he'd do ninety meetings in ninety days. He said he'd give me a break, move in with his brother. If it meant being with me forever, he'd do it. This time he would. I looked at the Alcoholic, at his pasty cream skin and thought, it's over. I am taking my life into my own hands. He found me when I was just rubble, stomped on me and ground me down. I used to be someone that didn't say no, but now, I am the person that did.

FAKE IT TILL YOU MAKE IT

He never came back.

It was a phone call; that's how he ended it. Read from a piece of paper written by his sponsor. Had someone else sum up his feelings.

"I'm born all over again. I'm learning how to crawl," he said. It has been three weeks since I sent him to AA. Now he's taking it one day at a time, doing ninety meetings in ninety days. He's admitted he's powerless over alcohol, that his life was unmanageable, that a power greater than himself will restore him to sanity. He's made a decision to turn his will and life over to God, as he understands Him, and is entirely ready to have God remove his shortcomings. He said he'd come back sober, but he left me for a room full of strangers who had twelve things in common. A bunch of anybodies in exchange for one me.

He says,

"If I stick with the bunch I'm gonna get peeled."

I say,

"I was the one that sent you there."

He says,

I thank my higher power for my sobriety, first things first, easy does it, live and let live, let go and let God. Yesterday is gone, tomorrow never comes, but today I will not take a drink. He's gonna keep going back because it works if you work it. If drinking doesn't bring you to your knees, sobriety will. Gratitude is attitude, he's gonna fake it till he makes it. He put the plug in the jug, because his worst day sober was better than his best day drunk. He said he is an instant asshole, just add alcohol. He's sick and tired of being sick and tired. It's easy to talk the talk, but you have to walk the walk. When you sober up a horse thief, all you have is a sober horse thief. It's a selfish program but you have to give it away in order to keep it and he's gonna stick with the winners because under every dress there's a slip.

He said, Daniel didn't go back to the Lion's Den to get his hat. The doors swing both ways. It's the engine that kills you, not the caboose. He suffers from Alcohol-ism not Alcohol-wasm. He says some people drink normally, he normally drinks. The price for serenity and sanity is self-sacrifice. One drink is too many and a thousand is not enough. Anger is but one letter away from danger. There is no chemical solution to a spiritual problem. He says he didn't get here drinking too much coffee, he has a disease that tells him he doesn't have a disease.

He came, he came to, he came to believe. The mind is a parachute it works better when it's open. He said, let it begin with him, he's sober n' crazy, he's gonna pass it on, it's in the book, he's just another friend of Bill W's. He's letting go of old ideas. He's keeping it simple, stupid. He is now positive that his drinking was negative, a journey of a thousand miles begins with the first step, he's responsible for the effort, not the outcome.

Seven days without an AA meeting makes one weak. Every day is a gift that's why we call it the present. AA has a wrench to fit every nut that walks through a meeting room door. It isn't the load that weighs you down, it's the way you carry it. The smartest thing an AA member can say is "help me." When you do all the talking you only learn what you already know. AA is not something you join; it's a way of life. There are no elevators, just steps.

He says he has another drunk left in him, but not another recovery. He is exactly where God wants him to be. Faith is a lighted doorway, but trust is a dark hall. He suffers to get well, he surrenders to win. From dependence he found independence. God will never give him more than he can handle. There are two days in every week which he has no control over: yesterday and tomorrow; today is the only day he can change. Courage is faith that has said its prayers. Depression is anger turned inward. Active alcoholics don't have relationships; they take hostages.

God grant me the serenity to accept the things I cannot change, courage to change the things I can and the wisdom to know the difference.

It was all bromide; he read it off like a script. Cranked out every aphorism known to man, maybe read me the entire Big Book. All I'm really aware of is he broke up with me over the phone at eleven thirty on a Thursday night. When he hung up, he took the phone off its hook. I heard the cries of the busy signal sobbing waah waah waah, but I never heard from him again.

BAD POEMS

I find myself in the next uncertain place.

My mother's house is cold; all the windows are closed. My old room is an office now, but it still smells of me. The pills will help you, take them one at a time, keep her in a room without scissors or razors, someone says, but I think it's me that spoke. I can't get dressed or out of bed.

The Alcoholic said, "I'm free." But he wasn't the one jailed. After six years, he ended me on the phone. No explanation, just the dial tone. He said he was a drunk when he met me, he's not a drunk anymore, how could he love me? His words were blah blah blah. Nothing made sense, but I felt the amputation. Still feel it now. He severed himself from me; I can feel him like phantom pain. I've been cut off, removed, still can't figure out what I did wrong.

She doesn't need to read the labels off the bottles. From the weight of it, she knows. Klonopin, Dilantin, Valium, Demerol. My mother knows; she always knows which pill to take. I fear she is trying to make me deader than I already am. If I were a cut, she'd ice me. She likes her pain on the rocks. But I have been numb for years and finally, I want my agony. I think of peeling back my skin, letting my important blood drain through the sheets. My mother's got medicine for every crisis, a drink for every occasion. It's a day, then a week, and I am still in bed. Some day I will be reduced to a page of type. Nothing more than a font of reminiscences at my funeral. Dates carved into a marble tombstone. I'll be recognizable only by the formidable fortress of mausoleum walls. What is the Alcoholic doing now?

In the daytime the phone rings off the hook, but it is never for me.

My mother comes and goes like a balloon, floating aimlessly in and out of doorframes. The wind takes her away every time she nears. She has dates and plans, and I am scheduled into her book once a day. She never stays, no one does. I am the only one who remains.

It rains all week and on Friday it storms. I get out of bed, watch the lightning ridicule the ruined sky. Take me, I think. Take me. I see myself tearing off my clothes, running out into a field under the epileptic night. Soldiered under a tree, I'll be front lines and fired at first. And as the lightning breaks me apart, I will finally see where I am: yet another place I was warned against.

The halls are long and my mother's room is dark and humid. There are photographs of my life with the Alcoholic stacked in piles on the floor. One is propped against a book and I pick it up, stare at the boy with the Jack rocks in his hand. He is wearing a suit that doesn't fit. Dampness clings to his face like a miracle. Party guests blur in the background like they don't count. A photograph captures nothing more than a dead moment.

The new therapist is New Age. She sits shoeless, legs crossed on a chair. She closes her eyes, arranges her mouth like she's humming. Books I will never read, Al-Anon testimonials, pamphlets, brochures, paper for garbage are placed into my bony hands. She does body work, but I feel molested. The incense is strong as a battle cry. The metallic clang of bells clears the negative energy around my head, but the sound stays with me for days like tinnitus. I see her twice a week. Afterwards, I always find myself crying outside of the nearest bank. The passers-by stare at me, think I'm homeless and toss me coins like a wish fountain.

In Al-Anon they all sound like Alcoholics. They call me names: addict, enabler, addict, enabler, but there is nothing able about me. I sit on a metal chair and write bad poems. They want to know my story. What is my story? I scour the floor for a thesis, but it's just cold concrete. Nothing absorbs it. I am my story. I sit on a metal chair. I write bad poems.

Dinner is leftover Chinese food, cold. Her favorite show is on, "Diagnosis Murder," but my mother puts it on mute and talks on the phone next to me. My apartment is empty and I think of returning, but I am scared to be alone. Here, at least, there is another body. The new therapist said,

"Even though he was with you, you were always alone."

I understand the sentence, but my brain won't wrap around the meaning. My mother is talking about me now. Barely trying to conceal the conversation. Her breath is overwrought, exaggerated. She expects pity from her listener, claiming the plight of her daughter as her own.

"Yes. No. Yes. I don't know. Um . . . I can't really say . . . maybe. She is. I know. And what about me? It's hard for me too, you know. Well what am I supposed to do about it?" I don't want to listen to her strained attempts.

Her bed is queen-sized and I sit on its edge. The photograph of the Alcoholic is at my feet, and I look at it from where I sit. It's changed somehow. There is something haunting about the picture now, as if the person caught were dead. That's how I see it, like he's lost his life and we are trying to preserve it. Mummify it in a frame. There is more weight on the bed—my mother.

"I love that picture of you," she says.

"What picture?" I ask.

"That one," she says pointing to the picture of the Alcoholic. She picks it up, presses her finger on a blur in the background. The oil on her finger marks the glass over the unfocused girl, over me. I squint, press the glass to my face and examine. I see then that it is me. A foggy gray wind. My face is faint underneath, like panty lines.

"It's so . . . you," she says.

"But you can barely see me."

"Well, I still know it's you."

"But, you can't see me."

"It's just that I like that picture of you, okay?" she says, hurt.

She gets up, walks to the door.

"God, I can't even give you a compliment," she snaps.

But it's not a compliment. It's savage, backhanded. As if she said, "You're getting prettier." She likes me best when I'm invisible. So do I, perhaps.

I lay the picture on my lap. My hair is a halo of gold and red, in need of a cut. My face is a charcoal drawing, smeared for effect, one feature blending into another. There is nothing distinct about me, not even my gaze. My eyes are holes, my nose sand, my mouth pepper. My dress is beige, hard to see where my skin starts and ends. I am words someone is mouthing, a hint. The oil stain from my mother's finger is still wet on the glass. X marks the spot under which I live. She'll take a wash cloth and wipe it away.

She stamped the pane like a passport. My ticket in, my ticket out. But the photograph is unsoiled. I turn it over, pop out the black cardboard and slip the photo out of its holder. I lay the empty frame on her bed, white billowy comforter. It sinks like bad luck. I wipe downy lint off the photo, wipe it clean on my shirt. I tuck my invisible self into the pocket of my shirt, guarding it like a bouncer.

This is the house I grew up in. If I stay, will I go back to high school, junior high, relive every bad experience that started and ended here? If I stay will I disappear into the margins of the original wood molding? When I bend down, the picture edge pricks my breast. I take it out, look again at her favorite picture of me.

In the basement the floor is cold. It ices my back through my shirt as I lay down, stare at the ceiling. The rusted sprinkler from Prohibition hangs pointless as foreskin. I am looking outside myself to understand who I am; I am getting nowhere, worse.

I walk from one end of the sidewalk to the other in the basement. At the far end of the basement is a door that leads to a large unused dark room. I remember this as my runaway place as a kid. I open the door, step in. The room smells stale, feels feverish. Alternately clammy and cold, as if it's been suffocating on it's own recycled air. I pull the damp light string. The bulb's heart breaks as it's switched on. It's a delayed reaction and five seconds after I pull the string the bulb moans, pouts, and then reluctantly peeks opens its eyes, unprepared for its own brightness, after such a long slumber.

The old enlarger is covered in thick sheets of plastic and dust. Decades old wedding presents are stored underneath the table top. In one corner, sleeping bags, and camping equipment, skis and stuffed animals are all haphazardly tossed together for life. In the other corner the contents of my old bedroom: clothes, year books, records, comic books, and movie posters. Near a discarded jug of developer lies a soggy cardboard Pony sneaker box. It's familiar; perhaps I dreamt it. Maybe a vision from my future. I kick the lid off, and inside everything is mine. Like a point expanding, I remember. My secret box from when I was twelve. 1985.

A twizzler, stale and hard to the touch. A hard white cube, shrunken and wrinkled, a marshmallow? A signed Lindsay Wagner picture, a love letter to Adam Ant, a Michael Jackson glove, a Rubik's Cube with the stickers peeled off and rearranged as if I solved it. A glow stick that won't glow, Bonne Belle chapstick (watermelon), a half-eaten candy necklace, and a wilted, war stained piece of paper. I unfold it.

MY LIFE PLAN

1. Get popular by eighth grade (be best friends with Kate Reissman). Get ears pierced?

2. Boyfriend by tenth grade (lose virginity!) preferably by Ricky Sundberg.

3. Switch schools, go to the FAME school.

4. Go to college. The one where Kate Reissman's sister goes. Cooper Union?

5. Study painting.

6. Fall in love. A painter, or sculptor. Maybe even my photography teacher who likes to take lots of pictures of ME!

7. Graduate. Everyone is proud. Get presents!

8. Leave home.

9. Get pretty (dye hair blonde??)

10. Make a lot of paintings, more than twenty.

11. Get a show at a gallery, maybe that one in Soho where we went with Mrs. Wheeler's class?

12. Travel. Go to all the art museums in far away places. Maybe see a real Modigliani and that guitar painting Picasso made, remember that one?

13. Sell your first painting by twenty-five. Make lots of money.

14. Buy a loft with the money.

15. Get married by 30. Maybe a carpenter who can build me lots of things, like a loft bed!

16. Have three kids. Name them: Ricky, Whitney and Marco.

17. Have a painting in the Whitney.

18. Get famous. Buy a dog. Name him, Alfalfa.

19. Buy a farmhouse. Grow vegetables.

20. Dress like an artist. Pants with stains and boots with spills on them, stuff like that.

21. Live everly after.

THE END.

I look at the list. I derailed at number five. I didn't study painting. I didn't fall in love with an artist; I fell in love with a drunk, a cliche. The paper is aged like I am. I put the list back in the box, cover it up with the Pony lid and walk out of the room. The stairs sag with each step I take back toward my mother. I close the door, walk down the hall. I can hear my mother scraping the leftover food into the garbage. Her complaints don't need voicing; you can hear them in her actions. One dish after another cracks as she throws them into the sink. The cupboards slam open and shut. No gesture is voluntary; every action is performed by the hands of a sacrificial victim; the cause: unknown. The house smells like a rain forest, but there is nothing peaceful here.

The ground seems endless as I walk back toward the box; the floor seems colder. I am closing in on possibility; my options are yellow, the smell of a spilling sun. I open the box, take the life plan out. As I put it in my shirt pocket I feel the photograph of the Alcoholic, of me, half erased, half thought-out. Acquire something new, shed something old. This is what I do. I exchange one article for another. Without bending I drop the photograph and it lands in the box, no effort. The life plan goes in my pocket and the cover of the box seals me with the Alcoholic into the past.

My old bedroom smells like stale toast. The bed is unmade and tissues lie in and around the wastebasket. Even though she is with you,

you are still alone. Orange rectangles stretch and increase from the center of my body. I find a pen, cross out numbers one through four.

I stand under the doorframe watching my mother in the kitchen, a rag tossed over her shoulder, hair like wool fraying at the ends. She slams off the faucet looks for something to wipe her hands on. Over the sink, under the sink, near the stove, nothing. She is frustrated, rolling her eyes and curling her lips as if this ultimate inconvenience will finally do her in. She can't see the rag across her shoulder, can't feel its presence even though she was the one to put it there. She peers under the table, opens the oven. Nothing. Finally, and with proper disdain, she wipes her hands on her skirt, loudly sits down at the table, opens the paper, takes a drink, a drag off her cigarette. The cloth will stay there until she changes for bed, she'll be annoyed when she sees it, but she won't take the responsibility for her own flightiness. For the fact that it was right there the whole time.

The sun hasn't gone down yet, and the streets are scorched with foreigners. On the corner of Mercer and Houston Street, I take out my list, take out my pen and draw a thick line through number eight. Leave home. Done. Crossed out. I'm gone.

EVERY STEP THEY MAKE

The Alcoholic is the first of my peers to get married. He met her in Alcoholics Anonymous. My friend heard she's a recovering crack and heroin addict, but I think she's just trying to make me feel better. It's three years after the breakup and I am in a jean store with my sister. We're waiting to pay when I see him in the line perpendicular to ours. He is eggshell white.

I notice these other things: his shoes are trendy, his jeans are too big, and the leather jacket he borrowed from me and never gave back hangs on his newly sober body. One strap of that same old knapsack hangs off his right shoulder. His wife puts a credit card on the counter, pays. He stands to the side of her, blocking her face from view. His right hand clasps her arm; the left clutches her pocket. He gobs on to her, gripped with fear she'll run away, break free if he lets go. It seems to take all his energy, but he holds on to her, like she's a life raft, his personal rescue. I recognize the grasp as much as the expression. He's in a daze, a type of wide-eyed trance. His eyes are fixed on nothing, some remote spot no one else can see. His pupils are dilated and he sees everything in double image. He looks extraterrestrial.

I am in a poorly directed, late-night Melissa Gilbert movie. One in which the person you think is dead is, in reality, alive and well and married to someone else. The Alcoholic hangs on to her the way he did me. All that matters, it seems, is that someone cares for him, assures him they won't leave. It's been three years thinking off and on about him. Portraits of him hang in my head. Sometimes I paint over them; other times I frame them, curate him like a gallery show.

He is living a brand new life, although the life we had together never really ended. The color drains from my skin. My sister keeps asking me what's the matter.

"It's him," I say. "It's the Alcoholic."

At the word alcoholic he snaps out of the trance, turns, sees me. He lowers his head a little, lifts his eyes, and gives me an almost apologetic smile. He quickly drops his hands from his wife, like this is a stick up. If only I had a gun. I don't return his smile, although I almost soften when I see his dimples. I pull my sister as the Cashier yells, "NEXT!" My sister has to sign the credit card slip for me, take the appropriate copy. I can't hear what anyone is saying. Everything pounds, like I'm in the mouth of a generator.

My sister takes my hand, leads me out the store. Outside, I'm a mannequin. Once, I readied a speech for this occasion, but I forget it now. My comebacks, one-liners, dart out of view like a cockroach before you can kill it. All I have is fight. Do I punch him? Push him into traffic? I consider switching my ring to my married finger, shoving it into his face, and saying, "me too!" I want to shear his face clean of that complacent glaze. It has been three years since he took me off his hook and now I want revenge. I want to wait for them, to see the wife. I want a good look.

Once outside, I take my sister's cell phone, pretend I'm talking so that my waiting isn't so obvious. I feel like a fool, talking into the receiver with no voice on the other end, but I can't leave. Not until I see her.

It's another few minutes before they emerge. She is first down the steps. As she descends, I try unsuccessfully to see her face. I can't see her features because all I notice is her bulging stomach, her pregnant belly. She is about seven months. They are having a baby. The Alcoholic is going to be a father. I am temporarily shocked into that sophomoric selfishness, the feeling that his being married and her being pregnant precludes me such fortunes.

At the curb she turns slightly toward the traffic light. I see her face then, her profile. Her cheeks distend farther than normal and her square head sits on her broad shoulders like a safe deposit box. It makes sense to me now, why people have been calling her Horse Face. They stand on the corner waiting for the light to change. He holds her elbow as if it was a cane and she holds a shopping bag in each hand. She is seven months pregnant, carrying not only their child, but also their baggage.

She will wake up to nurse the baby, soothe the baby, but the Alcoholic will sleep. During birth he won't know what to do; he'll find a way to make her care for him while she forces their child out into their life. He's always wanted a mother, someone who will love him unconditionally, and here he's gone and made one. I see her life in fast forward: running between two children, making certain they're clothed, fed, loved, safe. Racing to the nursery to comfort a newborn child, racing into the bedroom to soothe her deficit of a husband. Who will take care of her?

The longer I watch them, the clearer they become. It is as if I am staring at a magic eye drawing, the one where the young girl becomes an old woman, because what emerges from the background is all I can see. It's as obvious as a skyscraper. The hamster cage is steel, its vertical bars just wide enough for their heads to get caught between. Their only hope of escape is through the aid of another hand.

They don't know that they're in there, but I do. If I could break one of them out, it'd be her. But it's not my job to save her. It's not my job to save anyone.

As they cross the street, he pulls the other strap of his knapsack onto his shoulder. In bold letters, across his pack, is a bumper sticker: I HAVE A FRIEND IN JESUS. My sister cringes and I flinch, and then out of nowhere, we laugh. She snickers with superiority, a haughty advantage of her own independence. And I laugh, not with authority, but with humiliation at being linked to this person, this AA fiend, this Jesus freak. I imagine his apartment with Horse Face. Crucifixes of different sizes affixed to every wall; handwritten aphorisms over their desks: Let Go and Let God, Easy Does it, Live and Let Live; sheets and bedspreads with silk-screened nativity scenes; Laminated Jesus playing cards. In their closet: tee-shirts that exclaim, "I'm a friend of Bill W's!" In their kitchen, under the sink, a neatly folded AA annual picnic blanket. I can't bear to imagine their baby's room.

He doesn't tell her about me. I know he doesn't tell her I am there, because as they are crossing the street, he is the only one to look back. I wonder if she knows about me at all. Maybe he buried us all, the people who were his family before AA. Perhaps we've always been dead. When they get to the next store they're going to, he turns and looks at me, but she doesn't. For a moment I catch a sorrow in his eyes, a despair that belies the seemingly happy circumstances of his life. It's as if he's waiting, waiting for me to fetch him, waiting for my sister to ferry him some place safe. No matter his situation, I realize, he will always crave for the things he's been deprived of. His wife doesn't seem to notice he's not looking at her, doesn't seem to notice the undercurrent of hopelessness that is so apparent to me, my sister. She just keeps talking and talking, ignorant that she's completely alone. Ignorant that the woman who almost became his wife is standing right there, emancipated and seeing clearly now, for every step they make.

Photograph by Steve Wiley

AMANDA STERN was born and raised in Greenwich Village. Her work has appeared in *The Sunday New York Times Magazine, St. Ann's Review, Salt Hill, Spinning Jenny, Hayden's Ferry Review, Scriptum* (Netherlands), *Die Kroneitzung* (Austria), on *NYToday.com* and on the Oxygen Network. She spent several years working in independent film, assisting Ted Hope, James Schamus, Ang Lee, Terry Gilliam, and Hal Hartley. She has been a professional comic, a janitor, an archivist, an internet radio talk show host, an official partner on tour with the Cirque du Soleil, and a teacher. She recently edited a book for the Talking Heads box set and runs the Happy Ending Reading Series on the Lower East Side. She is the recipient of the Joan and John Jakobson Scholarship for the Wesleyan Writers' Conference. She is working on her second novel and lives in New York.

www.amandastern.com